But Jasper Came Instead

Christine Nostlinger

Translated by Anthea Bell

Andersen Press · London

Andersen Press Limited,
20 Vauxhall Bridge Road,
London SW1V 2SA

First published in English in 1983.
This translation © 1983 by Andersen Press Limited
Originally published in German in 1982 as
Das Austauschkind
by Jugend und Volk Verlagsgesellschaft m.b.H., Vienna,
Austria.
This edition first published in 2000

British Library Cataloguing in Publication Data available
ISBN 0 86264 987 0

Printed and bound in Great Britain by Guernsey Press
Company Limited, Guernsey, Channel Islands

Cover illustration by Julie Dodd

WHAT HAPPENED FIRST

My name is Ewald Mittermeier, and I'm thirteen years one week old at the beginning of this story. At the end of the story, I'll be thirteen years seven weeks old.

If I get our German teacher right about the difference between fact and fiction, this isn't really a story at all, because it actually happened to me. I'll try to keep it short. I'm not too sure I can manage that, because the six weeks I'm going to write about were very eventful, exciting weeks for me and my family. And I'm not used to writing about exciting things, because nothing exciting ever *did* happen at home before. (If I had to write a composition at school called, say, 'A Sunday At Home', I used to have to invent something, because a real Sunday at home wouldn't have filled up enough space for a composition.) My mother says that's because of our harmonious family life. My sister says she's wrong, and we don't lead a harmonious family life at all, just a boring one.

Well, whichever of them is right, I'm used to things being dull and ordinary, so I'm not much good at writing about exciting events. As I've just this moment noticed, because now I realize I can't begin the story a week after my thirteenth birthday at all. I have to begin it at least five weeks earlier.

It was the mid-morning break at school, on a Friday. I was sitting at my desk in the classroom, eating an apple which I wasn't enjoying very much, because it was a woolly apple and all brown round the core inside. Then

Herbert Pivonka, who'd been to the toilets, came back into the classroom. As he passed my desk, he said, 'Hey, Elsi, your mum's out there in the corridor talking to the English teacher.'

There are some people in my class who think it's terribly funny to call me Elsi. What happened was that they once saw my birth certificate, so they found out all my Christian names: Ewald Leonhard Stefan Isidor. And unfortunately, Wolfgang Emberger discovered that if you put the initials of all those names together you get a girl's name, Elsi.

I have these four Christian names because my mother wanted me to be called Ewald, after her brother, and Granny wanted Leonhard (I don't know why), and my father and Grandmother wanted Stefan. (*I'd* like to be called Stefan as my first name too.) The frightful 'Isidor' is after my Great-Uncle Isidor. 'We thought he'd like that,' my parents say. The fact is, Great-Uncle Isidor is rather rich, and if we do things he likes often enough he might leave us something in his will. (But all my boy cousins have Isidor for their second, third or fourth names too, so I don't suppose *I* have any chance of a legacy simply because of that stupid name.)

'What's the English teacher want to see your mum for?' Herbert Pivonka asked me.

Now, you could bet your life the English teacher did not want to see my mum! But more than likely my mum wanted to see him! About giving me a good mark for English in my report. This was only a month before the end of term, and my marks for the year's work were pretty well fixed by now. I'd be getting almost all Ones and Twos, meaning Very Good or Good, so it would be a good report. Except that in English, according to my homework marks, I was somewhere in between Two (Good) and Three (Satisfactory). And as I wasn't any kind of genius at oral English either, my own guess was that I'd get Satisfactory.

My mother just loves good reports. I think if I or my sister came home with a report saying nothing but Very Good for every subject, she'd like that even better than a black wild mink coat, even though a black wild mink coat is one of her dearest wishes.

Anyway, it looked as if my mother had come to see the English teacher to ask him to give me a Two (Good). So there wouldn't be any unsatisfactory Satisfactory messing up my report. She hadn't actually told me so, of course, but I know my mum! I saw it all at once. Naturally I didn't tell Herbert Pivonka. I couldn't tell a single soul in our class a thing like that. I mean, it was so silly! There were at least five people in the class who were terrified of English tests, and two who were sure to get Unsatisfactory in their reports.

So I pretended to Herbert that I hadn't the faintest idea why the English teacher wanted to see my mother, and meanwhile I was hoping fervently that the English teacher would stand firm and refuse to give me a Good. Because that wouldn't be fair, and I didn't want any presents in the way of good marks! Other people in the class are bound to notice that sort of thing, and then you're unpopular, and everyone thinks you're a swot or a teacher's pet, and that's about the last thing I'd like to be!

Back home at lunch-time my suspicions were confirmed. My mother admitted she'd been to see the English teacher to try and get a Good out of him, and she was annoyed because her cadging hadn't got her anywhere. 'I can't make it out,' she wailed. 'He's usually so sensible and understanding! He must have been having an off day!'

The English teacher had not been having an off day. You can bet he'd been feeling fine until my mother descended on him in the corridor at break. I know he can't stand having mothers come up to him and bother him with questions about our marks while he's munching his sausage roll. He's often told us so. 'What's the Parents' Evening supposed to be for?' he says. 'I call it outrageous and officious, people bothering me in my hard-earned break, and kindly tell your good parents so!' I did tell mine, too, but my mother just cannot imagine that the English teacher might be more interested in his sausage roll than my report.

So I sat down to lunch feeling relieved. We were having lunch in the kitchen. Mum and I eat in the kitchen when neither Dad nor my sister's at home. There was spaghetti and tomato sauce. I was just stuffing a forkful of spaghetti into my mouth when my mother remarked, 'He says we should send you to England.'

The spaghetti in my mouth made me speechless for a moment. When I'd got it down, I asked, 'Who says so?' (Of course I knew Mum meant the English teacher, but I can't stand her way of thinking out loud. I mean, for the last half-hour we'd heard no more of her trying to cadge a Two for me, we'd been talking about completely different things. How does she think everyone will know who she means when she just says *he*?)

'The English teacher, naturally,' said my mother,

8

looking at me and shaking her head. 'He said he was all for it,' she went on, 'because of your English accent! He says you're only in danger of a Satisfactory because your oral work's poor and you never put your hand up in lessons!' She sounded very reproachful.

I pushed my spaghetti plate away. I didn't feel like any more to eat.

Mum got up, fetched her handbag, and produced a sheet of pale green paper.

'A month's stay in an Oxford college, 15th July to 15th August,' she read to herself under her breath.

I knew what that pale green letter said. I'd had one of them in my school bag for weeks. They'd been handed out to all of us in class.

'There are still a few places free,' said my mother. 'I'll discuss it with your father this evening!' Then she put the green letter down on top of the bread bin on the kitchen dresser, stacked our dishes in the dishwasher and switched it on. And I'm certain I had gone white in the face. Greyish white, like snow in city streets. That's what usually happens to me at such moments. All the blood leaves my head, runs down into my stomach and simmers there, all bitter and boiling and bubbling hot. I mean, it really is infuriating when people never ask you what *you* think, or what *you* want, whether it's woolly socks, fountain pens, visits to England, the length of your underpants or where we're going out for the day. My mother knows what's good for me. And if she doesn't know for sure then she asks my father. She never stops to think of asking *me*!

This is a big problem in my life. I've often thought about it, and I've thought hard. All my thinking has led me to the conclusion that I probably don't stand up for myself enough. When I was at junior school there was a boy sitting next to me called Martin Hodina, who most certainly didn't have my problem. He used to howl when he didn't like something. He had a shrill, loud, high-pitched howl, like a factory siren at clocking-off time. His entire family were terrified of that siren howl, and people would ask him what he wanted three times, just to avoid the horrible sound of it. But it was too late to go in for that now. No use starting at thirteen! Anyway, if you're going to howl like that I think you need plenty of blood in your head. Martin Hodina always went bright red when he'd been howling, and as I mentioned before, on the kind of occasions when he howled, my own blood goes straight down to my stomach and simmers there.

My sister says I'm simply too good-natured and lazy to stand up for myself, but she can't be right. If I were really good-natured, my blood wouldn't be boiling away inside me. And it's my guess that a lazy person's blood just sloshes about inside his stomach, if it ever takes the trouble to run down from his head in the first place. But if I tell my sister this she laughs and says, 'Well, there's nothing for it, Ewald: you're one of those very rare cases of children who have been nicely brought up and it's worked! Nicely brought up children don't answer back!'

Maybe my sister is right. But thank heavens, I'm not so nicely brought up that I was letting them pack me off to an Oxford college without a word of protest!

I'm sure there are crowds of people who'd like to go and stay in one of these Oxford colleges. Five of our class had said they wanted to go as soon as we got the letter, and they were really looking forward to it. Three more were still trying to persuade their parents to send them. And two were very sorry they couldn't go on the trip to the college in England.

But personally, I didn't have the faintest wish to go and stay in an English college, with Dr Tannegeist in charge of us. And anyone who knows anything about me (which you would think might include my mother) ought to have known that too. I don't like going on school ski-ing courses, or school expeditions to spend a week in the country. I just do not like being with a whole lot of other schoolchildren all round the clock, with a couple of teachers in charge of us. At least there's one good thing about school ski-ing courses and weeks in the country: they may be no fun, but you miss lessons, and they're not much fun either. However, this trip to the Oxford college was to be in the holidays. I couldn't see anything but disadvantages: there'd be nasty breakfast, even nastier lunch, our free time all planned out for us, somebody snoring in a bunk bed above my head, our own dirty socks to wash, outings where we were counted both before and afterwards to make sure nobody was missing . . . and if you dropped behind a bit, or wanted to spend a few minutes on your own investigating the back of a church altar, they'd go on and on at you about not joining in and probably getting lost.

And so on, and so forth! It's bad enough having to put up with the teachers and the rest of our class six days a week all through the school year; I wasn't about to volunteer for more of the same in the holidays.

I tried explaining this line of thought to my mother that afternoon. My mother didn't see my point. She just went doggedly on saying how much a trip to Oxford would improve my vocabulary and accent, so that I'd easily get a Good or Very Good for English at school next year. She told me I was an ungrateful child, too. Not straight out, of course. My mother's not like that. She's always saying, 'You can't expect children to be grateful,' so she could hardly accuse me of ingratitude to my face. But she said, about ten times, 'Other children would be only too glad if their parents would send them to stay in England! After all, it isn't exactly cheap, and we're by no means so well off that we needn't consider the expense!'

And then, in the evening, my father was all for packing me off to England too. He wasn't so keen on my being able to say 'th' properly at school next year; it was my character he was concerned about.

'Ewald, you'll find this is a very worthwhile experience!' said my father, after the television news. 'A whole month away with your own contemporaries! What could be better, at your age? It's friends that matter most at your age, and you'll make real friends in Oxford! As you'll soon see, Ewald, a holiday trip like this is the ideal way of making friends!'

I might have known it, of course. Ever since I first went to nursery school, my father has worried about me because I don't have any 'real' friends. He keeps on and on at me about it. Apparently when *he* was a boy he always had at least four 'real' friends, and these four regarded him as their leader. Whenever he finds I still can't tell him I have any 'real' friends, he looks at me as if I were ripe for the psychiatrist's couch. He can't understand that I don't actually want any 'real' friends. He just thinks I can't get any. He thinks nobody wants to be friends with me. And the way he sees it, if nobody wants to be friends with me, there must be something wrong with me. And naturally that bothers him. He'd like to have a son who's all right in every way.

So in spite of my protests, my parents would have sent me off to Oxford just like that, if my sister hadn't come to the rescue. My sister Sybille is fifteen, and she's very clever. In fact she's brilliant. I don't mean her amazing short-term memory, which enables her to memorize something boring for a brief period, long enough to be tested on it and get a Very Good, and then forget the whole stupid thing again straight away. Sybille is the cunning sort of clever too. When she realized I was trying desperately and unsuccessfully to wriggle out of this trip to England she winked at me, and whispered that she'd try to get me out of it. I'll admit I wasn't very hopeful at first. But Billie is very crafty! She sat down opposite me and said, very loud, 'You'll be getting engaged to Verena in Oxford then, will you, Waldi? Isn't she the one you fancy?'

'Are you crazy?' I asked, but not too loud, because I could see Billie had something in mind.

Billie gently kicked my shin, and said, even louder, 'Ho, ho—you just wait, Waldi! That kind of thing goes on all the time when people go on these holiday trips to England. Crowds of them getting engaged every night at midnight, once the teachers are asleep! Last summer four people in my class got engaged, as you might say!' She chuckled quietly. 'That's why Gertrude is never going to be allowed to go to England again!'

Light was gradually dawning on me.

'Well, you never know,' I muttered, grinning and feeling extraordinarily silly. I mean, obviously something

13

of this nature does go on when there's a school trip somewhere in the holidays. At least, the people who've been on them say so afterwards. But much the same goes on during the school ski-ing courses and weeks in the country, and if the carryings-on are on the same level as the drinking bouts they can't be all that exciting. Once, when we were on a ski-ing course, Otto Werwenka smuggled in a bottle of vodka packed in his thick woolly socks, and some of our class drank it at midnight, sitting on the lower half of a bunk bed. Afterwards they had diarrhoea, and they were rather sick, but Otto and the others went on and on about it at school, right through till summer, saying what a fantastically trendy midnight booze-up they'd had during the ski-ing course. By the end of the school year it had turned into a positive orgy. A boy from another class even asked me if it was true everyone had smoked pot, and like an idiot I said yes, because they *had* been smoking cigarettes during the drinking party, and it wasn't until my sister explained that I realized pot was something different.

Since I'd just remembered about that drinking party, and since I'm not much good at talking about love and so forth, I told my sister, 'Anyway, you can bet there'll be some good booze around!' (Which is a daft thing to say, too, but Herbert Pivonka really did say it once, and he goes to one of these English colleges every year.)

So Billie and I went on with this sex-and-booze stuff for a good fifteen minutes, laying it on thick. If dear old Dr Tannegeist, who was escorting the Oxford party, had heard us he'd have collapsed foaming at the mouth with shock and horror. My mother had some trouble surviving our conversation too. She tried to interrupt, exclaiming,

14

'Oh, Billie!' and, 'Ewald, whatever do you mean, for goodness' sake?' and, 'I'm not having that sort of talk here!' But when she saw it was no use interrupting, because I can be relatively brave and even obstreperous when I'm with my sister, my mother left the room and slammed the door behind her.

At breakfast next morning, Mum told me that she and Dad had been discussing the trip to Oxford again, and on mature consideration they had both come to the conclusion that it wasn't a good idea for me to go to England.

'Why not, all of a sudden?' asked Sybille.

'He's too young,' said my mother.

'He wasn't any older yesterday!' said Sybille.

'He's never been away on his own,' said my father.

'Actually, he's been on the school ski-ing course twice and for a week in the country once,' said Sybille.

'But he hasn't been abroad,' said my mother. 'There's a great difference.'

'Especially when he doesn't really want to go,' said my father.

'But you didn't mind about that a bit yesterday,' said Billie, and I kicked her shin gently under the table, because it's not a good idea to overdo things, especially when you fiddled them in the first place. The main point was, I thought, that I wouldn't have to go to Oxford.

And my sister said no more, though perhaps that was because it was half past seven and time for us to leave.

On our way to school, Billie said, 'Sorry, but I can't help saying that kind of thing when I see the ridiculously muddled way Mum and Dad react to sex.'

'Most parents do,' I said. But Billie shook her head. 'Ours are even worse muddled than other people's,' she said. 'Other parents are only against sex for their own children. Ours can't even talk about it!' Other mothers and fathers, Billie told me, would just have said it was out of the question for their under-age son to spend his summer holidays necking in an Oxford college. 'But Mum and Dad,' said Billie, tapping her forehead, 'would go bright red and stammer with embarrassment if they had to say a thing like that, I swear they would! When it comes to sex they're totally speechless!' She glanced inquiringly at me and said, 'I mean, have they told you the facts of life yet?'

I shook my head.

'Well, there you are, then,' said Billie, triumphantly. 'They can't even bring themselves to do *that*!'

Just then Sybille's friend Irene Touschek came running out of a side street, waving to us, so I didn't get a chance to say any more about the facts of life. Actually, my sister wasn't quite right there. Dad had *tried* to tell me the facts of life, about a year before.

'I want to talk to you, Ewald,' he'd said one day, when he and I were alone at home. He looked as if he had very bad toothache. I was afraid something awful had happened. Perhaps Granny's dying, I thought. Or Grandmother. (Granny is Mum's mother, and Grandmother is Dad's mother.) Or we've lost all our money, I thought, and we won't even have enough to buy food, or go on holiday. Or perhaps we've got to move to another city. (That nearly did happen once, ages ago, because Dad was going to be promoted. But luckily somebody else in his firm got the promotion instead.)

16

I was enormously relieved when Dad finally explained that I had now reached the age when I ought to know about the sexual behaviour of Man. And being so glad neither of my grandmothers was ill, and we hadn't lost all our money, and we weren't going to move away from Vienna, and noticing how difficult Dad found it telling me about the facts of life—he was stammering like mad as he muttered something about strong drives, loving relationships and close embraces—I told him he didn't have to explain, we'd learnt the facts of life in school anyway. Which wasn't true. At junior school, we'd learnt about babies growing inside their mothers and how they come into the world, and the teacher had told us about little sperms joining up with eggs. But nobody had told us what a man and a woman actually do when they want to have a baby, and why they keep on doing it when they *don't* want to have a baby. I'd have liked to hear about that, but not from a father who was prowling the room like a lion with toothache, and couldn't utter more than two normal words at a stretch without adding three Ums, two Ers and a Well. It was horribly embarrassing. As bad for me as for my dad. And when I told my white lie, so as to put a stop to the whole embarrassing scene, he gave me a hundred Austrian schillings! In the normal way he doles out my pocket money every Monday, with a sigh, and if, as often happens, I can't manage on my pocket money, he lends me a few schillings with an even heavier sigh, and never forgets to subtract them from next Monday's money. So he must have been feeling immensely relieved if he gave me a hundred schillings just like that, for no reason at all!

Now I've gone and got right off the subject I was going

17

to tell you about, and I said I'd keep it short, so here goes again:

Things went on quite peacefully for over a week. If you're like me, and you have a good report coming, the last few weeks at the end of the school year are rather like a lukewarm bath: mild and liable to send you to sleep. Especially in the mornings. You doze off, waking up with a start now and then and wondering what on earth you're doing sitting there, and wishing you had understanding parents who'd write a sick note saying you had summer 'flu. Because it would be far more comfortable to lie in bed propped on one elbow and reading a book, instead of being slumped over your desk surreptitiously squinting past your elbows at the book on your knees, so that no one will notice it's not a textbook you're reading. At the end of the school year, other people in the class don't like that any more than the teachers do. I can see why. If you have to work really hard to make up the difference between Satisfactory and Unsatisfactory in a test, and somebody else is sitting there reading a science fiction strip cartoon book, you wouldn't feel good about it. But then, if I stare straight ahead of me, all grim and earnest, right through the test, it's not actually going to get the other person the Satisfactory he's after. And you can't prompt someone unless he's on the right track to begin with—*then* you can whisper to him, or point out a few things, and help him get a Very Good instead of a Good. But it's a sad fact that it just isn't possible to help the people at the bottom of the class who are going to get Fives (Very Unsatisfactory) anyway, even though they don't believe that. Once, I tried telling Herbert Pivonka during a geography test that they mine a lot of diamonds in South Africa, because he obviously didn't know. I can give him a hint, I thought, and happening to have a little pack of cards for playing patience in my desk I showed him one with diamonds on it. So Herbert looked at me, beamed, nodded and told the teacher, 'They make lots of playing cards in South Africa, sir!' And the whole class laughed, and Herbert Pivonka got his Five anyway.

So on one of those mornings like a lukewarm bath, during Maths, Lene Stollinka passed me a note. It contained the following, and as far as I was concerned utterly baffling, remarks:

'Is it Yes or No? My mum needs to know one way or the other. She rang your place hundreds of times yesterday, but the number was always engaged.

Lene.'

The one thing that didn't baffle me about this note was our phone being engaged. For the last two days Sybille and her friend Irene Touschek had been enemies instead. And another friend of theirs, Verena Haberl, had rung my sister yesterday to tell her what lies Irene had been spreading about her at the youth group. And then, still on the phone, my sister had told a fourth and then a fifth friend. And then Irene rang to say a sixth friend had told her what Verena had told my sister, and there wasn't a word of truth in it, she had not said that at all, she didn't go behind people's backs. And then my sister, still on the phone, told all her other friends about this call from Irene. So the telephone was in use the whole time.

At break I took Lene Stollinka's note over to her and said, 'What's all this about, Lene?'

'The Londoner, of course. Wanted or not?' said Lene. 'My mum really has to know *now* if the answer's yes or no, because if it's no she must write at once and say so.'

'What's a Londoner?' I asked, and Lene looked at me as if I were a feeble-minded baboon. But I honestly thought she must be talking about some kind of consumer goods I hadn't heard of before and known as a Londoner which my mother had ordered from Lene's mother, who works in a department store. If you order things from Lene's mother you can get a fifteen per cent discount.

However, by the time the bell went for the end of break, I knew Lene was not talking about a new kind of cookware, or an unusual tartan kilt, but a boy of thirteen who lived in London. A nice boy with dark hair, Lene Stollinka said. This boy had been coming to spend six weeks with the Stollinka family in the holidays, because Lene Stollinka's brother had spent six weeks with the boy and his parents last summer.

'A foreign exchange,' said Lene.

But now this boy couldn't stay with the Stollinka family after all, because Lene and Peter's grandfather had been very ill, and the family had to have him to live in their apartment, and the poor old man was in pain all day, groaning.

'The doctor said he won't get any better,' Lene told me. 'He may even die. So Mum said in the circumstances we can't have Tom to stay; it wouldn't be any fun for him. So *your* mum told *my* mum that perhaps you'd have him instead. This was the day before yesterday, when your mum was getting something from my mum!'

Lene was looking at me in surprise, because by now she realized this was the first I'd heard of any of it. She grinned, and said, 'Your mum said she'd be glad to have Tom come and stay, to improve your English accent!' It was obvious that she thought a woman who'd have a foreign boy to stay just to improve her son's accent was out of her mind.

'Well, we're not having him!' I told Lene.

'Oh?' said Lene. 'But how do you know? I mean, just now you didn't even have a glimmering you might be *going* to have him.'

'We're not having him because I don't want him!' I shouted.

Lene nodded a couple of times, whistled quietly, and then said, 'But it's not up to you, is it, Waldi?'

I turned and went back to my desk. Once again all the blood in my head had run down to my stomach and was seething away there. Seething even harder than usual! Because from the way Lene spoke, it sounded only too likely that everyone in our class knew how hard I found it to stand up for myself at home.

In the last break I went to see my sister in her classroom and asked her if she knew anything about this foreign exchange. She didn't, which was not surprising. She'd spent the last few days wearing headphones at home, except when she was telephoning. My mother doesn't like her to listen to music through headphones anyway. 'It must be bad for you, having that racket in your ears the whole time,' she says. 'It'll lead to softening of the brain and inability to concentrate!' But for the last few days my sister had been wearing her headphones even when she wasn't listening to music. She went around the apartment with the cable trailing behind her, just to show she wanted no part of our family life, and this simply infuriated my mother. A couple of times she even snatched the headphones off my sister's head and threatened to burn them. (Although we have central heating.) And once my mother and my sister actually fought for the headphones, and afterwards the metal band was bent out of shape, and my sister cried and told me she was going to leave home and get work abroad somewhere, looking after small children.

So my sister didn't know anything about this English boy either. All she *could* tell me was that Lene's story was probably true. Because before leaving the apartment that morning she'd heard my mother saying to my father, 'I must ring Frau Stollinka. Do you think it's all right to ring her at work or not?' And my father had said the days when you couldn't ring an employee at his or her place of work were gone, and a good thing too. (Naturally my sister didn't think this was anything important. She, too, had thought Mum wanted a fifteen per cent discount on something she was buying through Frau Stollinka. The fact is, Mum is mad on discounts. I suspect she sometimes buys things she doesn't need at all, just to get them on the cheap!)

To cut a long story short, Lene Stollinka was right. My mother *was* planning to ask this English boy from London to come and stay six weeks with us. When, through bloodless lips, I asked why I'd been left to hear about this from Lene, and why she hadn't told me before or discussed it with me, she said the first thing was to get in touch with Tom's parents by letter and telephone and make sure they agreed. They had to give the go-ahead if their son was to come and stay with a family other than the one where he'd expected to go.

This time my sister was no help, because of her craze

for the headphones. She wouldn't even take the stupid things off to listen to my protests. She just looked miserable and said, 'I couldn't care less, Waldi. I don't mind a bit if he comes or not.'

I think my sister was rather unhappy at the time over her quarrel with her friend Irene. As far as I could gather from the lengthy telephone calls (she did take off her headphones to telephone, of course), the reason for this quarrel was called Sebastian and was in Form 7b. Both my sister and Irene fancied this Sebastian. But horrible, underhand Irene had been telling everyone Billie kept chasing Sebastian, and had sent him a love letter! Whereas all my sister had actually done was give him a note from their piano teacher; they had the same teacher, and the note was to ask if Sebastian could change next week's piano lesson from Tuesday to Wednesday, or something like that. But Irene was telling everyone in their class she'd seen Billie draw a red heart with an arrow through it on the back of the piano teacher's note. If you have a girl friend who behaves like that to you, whether or not you ever actually did draw a heart with an arrow through it, I can quite see you'd be unhappy and take refuge in your headphones. Especially when you also have a mother who keeps talking about it, because my mother had overheard the phone calls. She's not the sort who'll go discreetly away when Billie or I are on the phone, not her! If she hears us telephoning she comes into the hall on purpose, and pretends she has to clean the mirror or tidy up the shoe rack. Sometimes she stands right next to the telephone and keeps saying, 'Phone calls cost money, so do keep it short!'

My mother had never liked Irene, and now she knew

Irene and Billie had quarrelled she kept on at Billie, saying she'd seen directly what a sly, sneaky creature that girl was, but of course no one had believed what she said! Well, she hoped Billie had learnt her lesson and would never speak to Irene again, and in future would take more notice of the advice an experienced mother could give her, and thus avoid disillusionment!

With this sort of thing going on, I'd probably have *glued* headphones to my own ears! (If I'd dared, and with me that's far from certain.)

So I was left alone with the blood boiling in my stomach and my heart very heavy. It wasn't just that I didn't want the English boy Tom hanging around, and it was infuriating to be lumbered with him when no one had asked my opinion. I had plans of my own for the summer!

Wonderful plans! Secret plans! And to be honest, plans I hadn't yet dared put to my parents. But now I thought the time had come.

So after supper that evening I told Mum and Dad how I'd been wanting, for ages and ages, to spend a few weeks alone some time. Really alone!

Granny has a tiny allotment with an even tinier summerhouse on it. Since her legs got bad with water on them, however, she hardly uses the allotment at all. It's too much trouble for her to get there, and gardening is hard work. Anyway, she doesn't care for the place since Grandpa died. She says everything on the allotment reminds her of Grandpa, and she gets very depressed there without him.

I'd been dreaming all winter of spending at least a month living alone on Granny's allotment during the summer. Just me and a pile of library books, some bread and dripping to eat, and Granny's gooseberry bushes and apricot tree, and nothing else at all!

However, it was a big mistake to tell Mum and Dad this. I was throwing away my very last chance of not having the English boy to stay!

'He really *is* going crazy!' cried my father. 'Spend the summer alone on the allotment? We've got a recluse in the making here!'

Mum was horrified too, and said she'd never allow it. Even if the English boy didn't come! For one thing, I was still much too young to look after myself, and for another, it just wasn't a normal wish for someone of thirteen. People of thirteen, she said, don't want to be on their own. And if people of thirteen *do* want to be on their own then it's abnormal, and it is no part of a mother's duties to encourage her children in their abnormality.

And Dad said, 'I'll have seven more foreign children come to stay before I let you go and live like a hermit on that allotment! If you're going to be so eccentric we must just get you used to having other children around, and that's my last word!'

When my father says something's his last word, then he means it. I've accepted that. If Dad says it's his last word, he genuinely is not prepared to discuss matters any further, and it isn't worth your while thinking up more objections, so you might as well save yourself the trouble. Even Billie agrees with me there. She knows that when Dad says something is his last word, that's a barrier you can't cross. So bearing this in mind, I said no more. I did something I'm very good at: I gave in.

Over the next week or so it was a slight comfort that Peter Stollinka, Lene's brother, who was friends with this

Tom from England, had solemnly promised me he'd look after Tom all the time he was here. He said he'd be glad to, as well, because Tom was a good guy. Rather quiet and reserved, polite and a bit of a bookworm—'But when you get to know him better you'll like him a lot,' Peter told me.

The way Peter saw it, Tom would really just be using us as a place to sleep, while he spent his time with Peter in the day.

And Peter gave me some letters Tom had written him to read. I must admit they were quite amusing. Tom wanted to learn German properly, so he always wrote the first page in German, but he went back to English on the second page of each letter. From these letters, you could gather that Tom collected beer mats and matchboxes, that he didn't have much trouble with his work at school, he wore a brace on his teeth, he was an expert on science fiction, he had a brother called Jasper, he sometimes went out into the garden in the middle of the night to look at the moon, and he had a cat called Sarah who used to watch him looking at the moon.

The letters made him sound quite nice, and I told myself things could have been worse. (As for my dream of the allotment, I had to be honest and admit to myself that it probably wouldn't have come off, even without Tom. So I tucked it away at the back of my mind and kept it there for next summer.)

A week before the end of term, we got two pale mauve letters, one addressed to my parents and one to me. I recognized Tom's small, round handwriting directly.

Tom's letter to my parents was just a few polite

remarks in German. They sounded as if some grown-up had dictated them to him.

His letter to me was very short too. There was a Polaroid picture stuck to the sheet of pale mauve paper, showing a dark, very good-looking boy. Underneath, Tom had written:

'This is me (just so you know what you've let yourself in for).'

My sister, who was friends with Irene Touschek again by now and had given up wearing headphones except when she was playing records, thought Tom looked nice in his photograph. She even sighed and said regretfully, 'What a pity he's only thirteen! If he was a few years older he'd be just the right age for me, and we could have a really good time this summer!'

I pointed out that my sister was only just fifteen herself, so there wasn't all that much of an age gap between her and Tom. I mean, among my parents' friends there are several married couples where the wife is two or three years younger than the husband, and they seem to get on fine. But my sister insisted that she wasn't interested in anyone younger than eighteen or nineteen.

'You see, women develop much earlier, Waldi,' she told me. 'And boys of our own age seem just like babies to us!'

Well, too bad! (I never laugh at my sister when she talks like that. Even very nice people like Billie can sometimes get bees in their bonnets, and I think one ought to be tolerant.)

My mother was preparing for Tom's arrival, working harder at it every day. Soon, every other sentence she spoke contained the name of Tom. She even brought home a coffee mug with TOM on it. She'd had the name done specially. 'So that he won't feel left out and he'll be at home straight away,' she said. Because we all have coffee mugs with our names on them to use at breakfast.

My mother changed my room right round. I have stacks of orange boxes painted blue along one wall of the room, to make a storage unit four metres long and one metre high, and I keep all my things in these boxes. My mother re-stacked them so that they were only two metres long but two metres high. And she put the old bed from the attic along the two free metres of wall, and painted that blue. She even went to the big shopping centre to get Tom a bedside table and a blue bedside lamp. And she took half my clothes out of my wardrobe— the winter half—and put them in the hall cupboard to make room for Tom's clothes. And she fetched the old kitchen table up from the basement of the apartment house, painted it blue as well, and put it by the window.

'So Tom can have a desk,' she explained. 'He reads a lot, or so Frau Stollinka said, and I'm sure a boy who likes reading likes writing too.'

I can't honestly say I felt too happy with my room after Mum had rearranged it.

Every morning and every evening, my father asked if I'd written to answer my 'new friend Tom's nice letter' yet. I didn't actually think it called for an answer, but Dad went on at me so long that I wrote an answer, to keep him quiet.

The letter I sent to London was a remarkably silly one. My father dictated it. First he took a photograph out of an album; a picture taken last summer. It shows a cross on a mountain peak, with a lot of cloudy sky behind it. My father is leaning against the cross, my mother is leaning against my father, and I'm sitting in front of them. We're wearing anoraks and mountaineering hats.

My father stuck this picture on a sheet of notepaper, and I had to put numbers beside us in the photograph and write underneath:

1—My father
2—My mother
3—That's me!

(My sister Sybille, called Billie, was taking us up, that is the ground, why you cannot see her!)

I wrote this ridiculous nonsense down with a perfectly straight face, just the way he dictated it to me. Well, I was saying to myself, if my dear father thinks his command of English is perfect, let's not shatter his illusions!

Then my father dictated the following:

'Dear Tom
we are all glad to meet you next week on sunday. We have everything prepared for you. We hope that you will feel very well by us.
Your friend Ewald and his parents and sister!'

I wrote this down without comment too, and said nothing at all when Dad went on to tell me that modern languages, and especially English, had been his favourite subject at school. I just put the letter straight into its envelope and stuck it up, because I was afraid Billie might come into the room and get a sight of Dad's weird and wonderful English. She is not as tactful as I am. She'd have started giggling, and shown Dad where his English was wrong, and then his feelings would have been hurt.

And I expect I'd have had to write the letter all over again.

Otherwise, nothing much worth mentioning happened before the Sunday we were going to meet Tom at the airport. Unless you think my birthday's worth mentioning. In a way my birthdays *are* worth mentioning, if only for the fact that I've never yet had anything I wanted for a birthday present. This particular birthday, I got a pile of non-fiction books from Dad, on astronomy, on nuclear fission (four volumes), on native European plants and on cave paintings. Mum gave me a machine washable, striped blue and white summer suit. Granny gave me six pairs of underpants and six vests, one size too large. Grandmother gave me six pairs of socks, two sizes too small. (She forgets I'm still growing and last year's shoe size is never right.) And I hadn't wanted non-fiction books, never mind what they were about, or a suit, never mind what colour, or any underwear and socks, whether too large or too small! Though to be honest, I really did like Billie's present. She gave me all the Flash Gordon books published so far. She'd got them cheap from Irene Touschek, because Irene was broke at the time. However, even this magnificent present didn't feel quite right. There was something slightly suspicious about it, i.e. the name OSCAR TOUSCHEK stamped in large letters on the second page of each book. This is Irene's brother's name. It was possible that Oscar gave Irene the Flash Gordon books, or it was possible he'd been broke too and sold them to her. But I still have my suspicions. I can just see Irene turning up at our place some day looking embarrassed, and stammering as she admits she nicked her brother's Flash Gordons, and please would I give them back or she'll be in dead trouble at home!

Oh yes, and of course we had our school reports before the Sunday we were due at the airport. Dad was very pleased and thought they were fine, and he gave Sybille a hundred schillings for each of her Ones and fifty schillings for a Two. I got the same. And he said that although he wasn't really in favour of handing out cash for good reports, it seemed to be usual nowadays, so he wouldn't be the odd one out.

However, Mum looked sadly at my Satisfactory for English, and sighed. And Billie's report really annoyed her. Because Billie had One for everything except Art, and she got a Two for Art.

'It's a shame,' said Mum, 'a crying shame! That Art mistress must have something against you—spoiling your lovely report with a Two like that!'

I said, and Billie agreed with me, that my sister had no talent for Art whatever. And she was extremely lucky to get a Two! Billie can't even draw a proper line; all her lines look furry, because she makes them by joining a lot of little lines together.

'Well?' said my mother, not in the least impressed.

Billie tried explaining. 'Honestly, not long ago I drew a cow,' she said, 'and everyone else in the class thought it was a dog—a large dog!'

Mum was not impressed by this either. She said she already knew that Billie was no artistic genius. But when you have Very Good for every other subject on your report, she insisted, then you ought to get Very Good for Art too. 'After all, Art doesn't matter!' she cried.

31

I could see Billie getting cross. My mother didn't notice. 'In the autumn I'm going to go and see the Art mistress and ask her what she's got against you!' she went on.

'You dare!' cried Billie. 'You'd just make me look ridiculous!'

'I certainly will dare!' said my mother. 'I call it quite disgraceful to give you a Two for an unimportant subject like Art!'

Billie was fighting for breath. 'Talk about illogical!' she spat. 'First you say my mark for Art doesn't matter because Art's not important—so why are you getting all worked up about it?'

'Because it spoils your report, of course,' said Mum.

And Billie jumped up, glaring at her, and shouted, 'You're a pervert, that's your trouble! You go chasing good reports like a rubber fetishist after a pair of galoshes!'

Then she ran out of the room.

Mum watched her go, looking very angry indeed, with a frown on her forehead and the corners of her mouth turned down.

'I go chasing what like who?' she asked me. 'What's all this about galoshes?'

I shrugged my shoulders, pretending I didn't understand Billie's parting shot. Then Mum's face cleared, the corners of her mouth came up again, and she told me, in quite a nice voice, 'You know, Ewald, she's only cross because she really feels furious about that Two for Art as well, only she won't admit it. She's too proud! But I know Billie, and you mark my words, she's ambitious!'

At moments like this I always feel very sorry for Mum. It's a poor look-out when you're so extremely wide of the mark, and so very far from understanding what it's all about!

On the Sunday we were going to meet Tom, the second Sunday after the end of term, nothing at all went as planned. We'd been told to fetch Tom from the airport at 15.10 hours. So my parents had decided to start out at twelve noon. The fact that my parents were allowing three hours to get to the airport is not, as you might think, because we live a long way away, but because they're terribly unpunctual. Unpunctual the wrong way round, I mean. They always get everywhere far too early, which if you ask me is just as unpunctual as the usual way, arriving too late.

The idea was that we'd take Peter Stollinka to the airport with us, so that when Tom arrived from England he'd see a familiar face and wouldn't feel so strange and homesick.

Punctual people would have worked it out this way: it will take fifteen minutes to drive to the Stollinkas', then another five minutes to get Peter sitting in the car, and then it's three quarters of an hour's drive to the airport, so assuming we want to be there ten minutes before the plane lands, we'll need an hour and a quarter in all.

But my parents don't do things like that. They remember that there might be a traffic jam somewhere between us and Peter Stollinka's, or ten diversions, or a bad accident blocking the road. And then they say it's not certain Peter will be ready when we arrive, he might keep us waiting. And all the traffic lights might be against us on the way to the airport. And suppose there was a demonstration somewhere? We could easily lose half an hour just sitting in the car waiting for the demonstrators to march past. And planes have been known to arrive early, and then poor Tom would be standing around feeling lost.

We have to take this kind of thing into account, say my parents. So they add on ten minutes here and five there and fifteen there—and they end up allowing three hours for a seventy-five minute drive.

But anyway their miscalculations came to nothing, because things didn't turn out like that. First thing on Sunday morning Frau Fischer rang us up. Frau Fischer lives next door to Grandmother (that's Dad's mother). Frau Fischer said Grandmother was not at all well, and we'd better come round and see to her. She was calling from a phone kiosk, because neither she nor Grandmother has a telephone, and the line was a bad one. More than half of Frau Fischer's schilling's worth of time (and she didn't want to spend another schilling) was used up on saying, 'Hullo, can you hear me?' and, 'Sorry, I can't make out what you're saying.' In any case, Mum and Dad were very worried. And Dad said that even though it wasn't at all convenient today, we must call and see Grandmother. So we set off for Grandmother's very early. Billie was staying at home, but we picked up Peter Stollinka directly, because Mum wanted to drive straight from Grandmother's to the airport.

Grandmother lives on the outskirts of the city, in an estate house with a little garden behind it. Dad often says she shouldn't really be living alone any more at her age, but Grandmother doesn't want to go into an old people's home, and she's told Dad that if she ever has to leave her house and garden she'll wither away like a flower that hasn't been watered.

We reached Grandmother's just before eight. I had to shake Peter Stollinka awake. He'd gone to sleep in the car beside me. In the holidays he always stays up late, watching television until close-down, if he isn't planning to do anything next morning. And he couldn't have known we were going to call for him so early. That was why he was dressed in such an odd way, too. In his haste he'd put his jeans on over his striped pyjamas, and he was wearing one green sock, and had grabbed one of Lene's white knee-length socks instead of its pair. The T-shirt he was wearing looked like one of Lene's too, because it was so small and tight. And his striped pyjamas showed at the V-neck and below the short sleeves of the T-shirt. But Peter Stollinka is OK, and he wasn't cross. He fell asleep against my shoulder in the car, muttering peaceably, 'Couldn't care less if it's my old grandpa's death-rattle or your old grandmother's death-rattle I'm off to hear!' (Which sounds rather heartless when I write it down, but Peter didn't mean it like that. I know he's fond of his grandpa, and I don't think he has anything against Grandmother either.)

Grandmother was lying in bed under her thick white quilt, and she really did have a rattle in her throat, just as Peter had predicted. I didn't go close to her, because when Grandmother's in bed she never has her teeth in, and her face without her teeth is rather scary. Her mouth looks like a funnel with folds all round it.

Mum tried asking Grandmother some questions, to find out if she was seriously ill. Because Grandmother has a bee in her bonnet: she refuses to waste any food. She eats absolutely everything she's bought. Even if it's more than her small stomach can cope with. Even if it doesn't smell good any more, and it's gone the wrong colour. Sometimes that makes her sick, but it's not exactly dangerous. However, if her high blood pressure makes her ill that *is* dangerous. When she's sick because of something she ate, camomile tea will cure her, but if it's her blood pressure you have to send for the doctor. However, as my grandmother will never admit to having eaten stale old food, because she's afraid my parents will be angry, it isn't too easy to find out whether camomile tea will cure her or whether we ought to call the doctor.

This particular time, Mum decided on camomile tea, and an hour later, when Grandmother was still groaning and there was still a rattle in her throat, Dad decided on calling the doctor. He came, too. And he came back two hours later. He was a doctor on emergency call, because it was Sunday. He said Grandmother's stomach was swollen, and sensitive to pressure above the gall bladder. Grandmother admitted to the doctor on emergency call that she'd eaten five pieces of bread and goose dripping. The doctor on emergency call gave her an injection for now and some pills for later, and he told my mother that old people were a real headache.

When the doctor on emergency call had gone, Mum gave Grandmother a long lecture about healthy nourishment in old age. Grandmother pulled the quilt up over her head. Dad told Mum she was wasting her breath and she might as well leave off talking. Mum did, and then she began cleaning Grandmother's little house. Peter and I helped her. Dad went into the garden and pulled up weeds.

But Grandmother was not at all pleased to have us cleaning up. She came out from under her quilt again and was cross. Apparently we were getting everything mixed up. She said a lot more too, but I couldn't make it out, because she didn't have her teeth in, and without her teeth she hisses terribly. When Mum was about to throw five used coffee filters out Grandmother got furious, and shouted, 'Leave those filters alone! They're going on the garden for fertilizer!' She wouldn't even let Mum throw some squeezed lemon halves away.

'I'm going to make lemon essence out of them!' Grandmother protested.

'But they've gone all mouldy,' said Mum.

'I'll scrape the mould off,' said Grandmother.

'Yes, and make yourself ill again, so the doctor has to call and we have to look after you!' snapped Mum.

Grandmother sat up in bed and hissed, bitterly, 'Nobody has to look after me! *I* didn't ask you to come! I can't help it if that stupid Fischer woman rang you!' And then Grandmother threw her tin mug at the wall. It still had quite a lot of camomile tea in it. I don't know whether she meant to hit Mum with the mug. Afterwards, Mum claimed she did. So did Peter Stollinka. Anyway, I enjoyed it. Usually I like Granny better than Grandmother, probably just because I know Granny much better. When I was little I spent quite a lot of time at Granny's, and I only went to see Grandmother every other Sunday. But you can't help liking someone who throws tin mugs about the room when she gets cross! It was most impressive. Even the funnel-like mouth didn't scare me any more. Grandmother sat there in bed like an avenging goddess, a very old one, and I thought even her thin, white, shoulder-length hair was standing out on all sides like Struwwelpeter's in her rage.

Mum's feelings were hurt, and she went out to join Dad in the garden. Peter and I stayed with Grandmother. Grandmother said she was feeling better now and she'd have a little nap, because what with the pain in her stomach she hadn't been able to sleep last night. So then we went out into the garden too. Mum sent me to the phone kiosk to call Billie and tell her Grandmother wasn't seriously ill. I went to the kiosk with Peter, but our number was engaged. We tried about five times, but we never got through. And since I didn't think the message I was supposed to give Billie was all that important, I went back to the garden. By now it was mid-day. Mum said she didn't see why she should stay watching by the bed-side of a nasty-minded old woman who flung mugs at her, and she wanted to go and get some lunch. Peter Stollinka was all for that too. His stomach had been grumbling loudly because he hadn't had any breakfast. Mum made Grandmother another pot of camomile tea, and as her feelings were still hurt I carried it upstairs and put it on Grandmother's bedside table. Grandmother gave me fifty schillings. She gave Peter fifty schillings too, which I thought was overdoing it. She got the money out of the drawer of her bedside table, and then gave me her cheek to kiss. I kissed it, reluctantly. Because of all her old wrinkles. I usually manage to avoid kissing Grandmother when I'm saying goodbye to her, but I'd come to like her so much better when she threw that mug that I managed to overcome my distaste for it for once. Peter Stollinka kissed Grandmother's other cheek, to thank her for the fifty schillings. Later, he told me he didn't mind wrinkled cheeks, but he'd never dream of kissing his sister Lene, whose cheeks are all spotty.

We went to a nice restaurant. Unfortunately it was almost two o'clock by now, and most of the best dishes were crossed off the menu. Except for fish, which none of us wanted, there was only shin of beef and goulash left. We didn't want shin of beef either, so we all ordered goulash. Mum was rather jittery. For one thing, in this rather posh restaurant she felt embarrassed about Peter's striped pyjamas emerging from the legs and arms and neck of his clothes, and for another, she was afraid the meal would take too long and then we'd be late getting to the airport. She wouldn't even let Peter and me have an ice in case we were late. And she almost started a fight with Dad, because in her opinion Dad had not called loud enough for the bill, and that, in her opinion, was why the waiter still hadn't brought it. So then Dad waved a five-hundred-schilling note in the air until the waiter noticed and came hurrying up.

We weren't late at the airport, of course; as usual, we were unpunctual the wrong way round. We stood for almost half an hour behind the plate glass in the Arrivals lounge, watching people who'd come off planes that were nothing to do with us waiting for their luggage. I got a kind of wanderlust. I felt I'd much rather have been handing in my case on the Departures side of the building and jetting up, up and away, not standing here wedged in among all the other people meeting children on a foreign exchange, waiting for Tom from England.

Finally they announced that the charter flight from London had landed, and a few minutes later a lot of children and young people came into the area beyond the plate glass. Peter Stollinka pressed his nose flat against the glass, watching the boys and girls making for the conveyor belt with their luggage on it. He kept muttering, 'Can't see Tom. Tom's not there! Tom can't have come!'

I tried being soothing. 'You can only see the backs of half of them,' I said.

But Peter claimed he'd be able to recognize his friend Tom even from his back view, even on a pitch dark, moonless night. 'No,' he said unhappily. 'Tom hasn't come!' Then, suddenly, he narrowed his eyes, like a very short-sighted person, and whispered, 'Oh no! Oh, mercy! I don't believe it!'

'What's the matter?' I asked. 'What's up?'

Peter's eyes were still narrowed, and he had one hand up to his cheek. He looked as if he were facing nameless horrors. My parents noticed his odd behaviour, too.

'Is something the matter, Peter?' asked my mother, worried.

'What is it, Peter?' asked my father, even more worried.

The luggage off the London flight was arriving on the conveyor belt beyond the plate glass now: bags and cases and rucksacks. First of all a bright red bag came rolling along. Its zip was only half closed, and all kinds of stuff was spilling out. Next came a rather battered, bright green case. And then a kind of tramp's bundle, fairly large, wrapped in a black and white check Arab headdress.

A fat, sandy-haired, freckled boy made for the conveyor belt. He grabbed the red bag and the bundle in one hand and the bright green case in the other, and then

40

waddled towards the exit and the Customs man.

Peter Stollinka looked blankly at me and my parents and said, in English, 'Oh, for heaven's sake—it's the dreaded Jasper!' (I suppose the shock had robbed him of the use of his native tongue, and awful memories of last summer had conjured up something people had said at the time.)

The boy he had described as the dreaded Jasper came into the Arrivals lounge, put down his three pieces of luggage, and looked round.

'Who's Jasper?' asked my mother.

'Tom's brother,' said Peter.

'Oh, is he coming on an exchange visit too?' asked my father.

'But where's Tom?' asked my mother.

Peter Stollinka shrugged his shoulders helplessly.

One by one, the London children were going through Customs, to be met by their host families. Several of them were gathering around two couriers by the exit. Probably they were people who hadn't been recognized by the families meeting them yet.

The fat boy called Jasper stood rock-like among the milling throng. He didn't even take any notice of several other children stumbling over the luggage he'd dumped on the floor.

I was rather fascinated by the look of this boy! I'd stopped looking for the missing Tom, and I was staring at Jasper. I saw him take something out of the back pocket of his jeans. A photograph, stuck on a piece of notepaper. He glanced briefly at the photograph and then round the lounge, not in a very friendly way. Then he saw us. First he nodded to Peter, not in a very friendly way either, then he picked up his case, his bag and his bundle in one hand and waddled over to us, all lop-sided because of his baggage. He stopped right in front of us, put his bags down again, and compared the three people wearing mountaineering hats in the photograph with Mum, Dad and me. Then he nodded to himself, and told us, 'I'm Jasper.'

'Where's Tom?' asked Peter Stollinka.

The fat boy gave Peter a very nasty look and said, 'He's sick. Broke his left leg. They sent me instead of him!'

'Oh, shit!' whispered Peter Stollinka, but so quietly that no one but me could hear him.

I don't think my parents specially minded the fact that Tom had broken his left leg and we had been sent someone called Jasper instead. Which made sense: I mean, all my father wanted was for me to make friends with other children, and all my mother wanted was to get me saying 'th' properly.

But I felt unhappy about it straight away. Whether because of Peter's horrified whisper, or whether I'm the sort of person who gets premonitions, I don't know.

Anyway, this was the beginning of our first day with Jasper, who'd been unloaded on us instead of his brother, and that was the start of the six weeks which are really the subject of my story.

JASPER'S FIRST THREE WEEKS

Sunday, 19th July

Mum and Dad were going to take Jasper's luggage to our car, but Jasper growled. He actually growled. Like a big dog when someone's threatening to take its bone away. Dad and Mum, alarmed, stopped being helpful. Jasper picked up his bundle, his bag and his case. Before he did so, he had simply dropped the sheet of notepaper with the photograph of the cross and the mountain peak on it, and Mum, with a kind smile, had picked it up. 'He's just rather confused still,' she told Dad. 'That's not surprising!'

When we reached the car, Dad opened the boot and Jasper put his bag and his case inside it. Dad was going to throw the bundle wrapped in the Arab headdress in after them, but it was too heavy to throw.

'Phew!' grunted Dad. 'What on earth has the boy got in there?' Panting, he heaved the bundle into the boot. 'It must weigh kilos!'

'That'll be his collection of stones,' said Peter. 'He usually takes it around with him.'

'A young collector?' said Dad. 'How interesting!' He smiled at Jasper and pointed to the Arafat-style bundle lying in the boot. 'Stones?' he asked in English.

Jasper said nothing.

'In Austria we have many stones,' Dad bravely pressed on, still in English. 'If you are interested in stones, you

43

will make eyes by us!'

Jasper still said nothing. He simply ignored Dad entirely. Dad sighed and got into the car. The rest of us got in too. Jasper was in front, beside Dad, and Mum sat in the back in between Peter and me. I wondered what an English boy would think Dad meant by saying, 'You will make eyes by us!' and I couldn't help grinning. Peter said, 'I can tell you, you'll soon have that grin wiped off your face!'

Dad tried telling Jasper something about the surroundings of Vienna as we drove along, speaking English to him. 'This is the big oil refinery,' he said. And, 'This is a little town named Schwechat.' And, 'This is Zentralfriedhof. All dead people of Vienna are living here!' Jasper didn't bother to look out of the window in search of all the dead Viennese people living in the cemetery. And when Dad said, 'Now we drive the belt along!' (by which he meant we were going along the Viennese road called the Gürtel, which literally means 'belt'), this announcement left Jasper cold too. He had produced a bag of peanuts from his jeans pocket. Peanuts in their shells. He started extracting the nuts and munching them, dropping the broken bits of shell on his well-filled trouser legs. Then he swept the peanut shells on to the black pile flooring of our car. I stole an interested glance at my mother. Keeping the inside of the car spick and span is one of the Ten Commandments in our family, and if my sister or I broke it Mum always used to go on at us, loud and long. But now she was still smiling, though there was a slightly frozen look to her smile.

'Peter,' said my mother, 'please will you tell Jasper to

44

stop eating peanuts? I've made a nice cake, and if he goes on eating he won't have any appetite left when we get home!'

But Peter shook his head. 'I'm not speaking to him except in an emergency!' he said, pointing at Jasper. 'We're deadly enemies, see? And anyway,' added Peter, with a pitying glance at my mother, 'he never does what you ask him to do. He always does the opposite!'

'Oh, come, Peter!' said my mother. 'It can't be that bad!' By now, her smile was definitely deep-frozen.

'Can't it, though?' Peter was staring grimly at the head-rest in front of him, and Jasper's shock of sandy hair on the head-rest. 'Send him back!' he said. 'You'll only have trouble with him!'

Jasper's head jerked away from the head-rest, Jasper turned round to look at us, put his head through between the front seats, stared at Peter and said in English, quite quietly but very clearly, 'Shut up, you bloody bastard!' Then he turned round again, leaned back, and devoted his attention to his peanuts.

My mother had gone white as a sheet. 'Oh, Peter!' she said quietly. 'I think he understood what you were saying!'

'Course he did,' said Peter. 'He's been learning German at school for the last two years, hasn't he?'

'Do you speak German, Jasper?' My mother leaned forward to the front seat. It must have been a big effort for her to speak in such a friendly tone to someone who'd just been so rude.

'No,' said Jasper. It sounded quite threatening, as if he meant: leave me alone or I'll hit you!

We drove the rest of the way home in total silence. We

didn't even speak as we got out of the car outside the apartment building. But when Dad put out his hand to pick up the heavy, Arafat-style bundle, Jasper growled again.

We live on the fourth floor of an old building. It's listed as being of historical interest, and it has no lift. There's a spiral staircase up to our apartment. We climbed it in single file, Jasper bringing up the rear with his baggage.

'Help him!' Mum whispered to Dad. 'It must be too heavy for him!'

'He growls,' Dad whispered back. 'If I touch his things he'll probably bite too!' All the same, he turned round and asked in English, 'Would you be so kind and give me a part of your things?' Jasper didn't reply, just shook his head and went on hauling his heavy load up from step to step.

'Please yourself,' muttered my father, and we went on upstairs. The distance between the rest of us, who had nothing to carry, and the heavily laden Jasper grew greater from floor to floor. By the time we reached the apartment, he was only on the second floor—or so I supposed, from the distant sound of panting.

My sister met us in the hall with the information that Tom's brother Jasper was coming to stay with us instead of Tom.

'How did you know?' asked Mum.

'I've been talking to the Pearsons on the phone for hours!' said my sister, rather proudly. The first telephone call from London, she told us, had come soon after we set off. It was Mr Pearson to tell her his son Tom had fallen downstairs last night, goodness knew how, and broken a leg, so unfortunately he couldn't fly to Vienna today. And not later, either, because you couldn't send a boy with his leg in plaster on a foreign exchange. Billie said Mr Pearson had said all sorts of other things, but he'd spoken terribly fast, far too fast for her own inadequate command of English, and there was a lot of crackling on the line too.

'So then I rang the Stollinkas, but you weren't there any more,' said Billie. 'And then Mr Pearson rang again half an hour later. He asked if we'd mind having Tom's brother instead of Tom. I think he thought I was Mum the whole time. He said they couldn't get their money back for Tom's flight at this stage—and *I* thought: well, what does it matter which brother comes? I couldn't reach you at Grandmother's, of course, and we had to decide fast. Did I do the right thing?'

At this moment a sound came upstairs and through the open front door: a deafeningly loud sound which went on for a long time, but gradually dying away. I should think a sizeable landslide on a rocky mountain would sound much the same.

'Jasper's collection of stones,' said Peter, unmoved. 'I was just thinking that Arab headdress wouldn't stand the strain much longer.'

'Ought we to help him?' asked my mother hesitantly.

'You want to be growled at again?' asked my father.

'What on earth are you all on about?' said Billie, running out of the apartment and downstairs.

My mother went into the kitchen to make coffee. My father went into the living room to lay the table. Peter and I stayed out in the hall by the door, expecting to hear a savage growl from the floor below. But there was no growl, just a lot of little clicking sounds, like stones being hastily thrown together in something.

47

Quite a while later—Peter and I were already sitting down at the table with Mum and Dad, having coffee—Billie and Jasper came into the living room. Jasper was lugging his Arafat-style bundle of stones along again; Billie was carrying his case and his bag. 'They went all the way down to the basement,' she panted, 'but we've found them all. He's got some lovely stones. Shaped like hearts and kidneys, and some with holes in them, and some with stripes! I didn't know there could be so many kinds of stones!'

'Do sit down, Jasper,' said my mother invitingly, pushing the chair she'd meant for him slightly to one side.

Jasper came over and sat down. His fingers were black as soot. The staircase doesn't often get washed, so if you pick up stones on the stairs you're bound to get your fingers dirty. Billie's were dirty too. She went into the bathroom, and we could hear water running.

'Jasper, your hands!' said Mum.

Jasper looked at his black fingers, and was obviously perfectly satisfied when he saw they were all there.

'They are dirty!' said Mum. Reproachfully.

But Jasper had lost interest in his fingers. He looked at the slice of Black Forest cherry cake on his plate. He pulled the plate towards him, examined the slice of cake closely, found a red cherry in the white butter-cream filling, dug it out of the butter-cream with two black fingers, and put it in his mouth. The fingers he was using instead of a fork went into his mouth too. When he brought them out, they were visibly cleaner.

'Jasper, go and wash your hands!' said my mother. Jasper stared grimly at her. My mother stared back. Jasper sighed, then took an Austrian Airlines refresher

48

tissue wrapped in foil out of his jeans pocket, tore the foil open and threw it on the floor, unfolded the tissue, and scrubbed at his hands with it until the tissue was dark grey. Then he crumpled that up and threw it on the floor too. My mother was watching in consternation.

'He always was a filthy pig,' Peter told her. 'And he never washes! He loses a layer of dirt in the summer if he bathes in the sea, and that's it!'

Jasper didn't drink any coffee. He reduced his slice of cake to crumbs so as to get at the cherries in the filling. They were all of it he ate. He left the squashed remains of sponge and butter-cream filling and whipped cream topping on his plate.

After coffee, Mum took Jasper to my room and showed him his bed and bedside table, and the empty half of the wardrobe.

Jasper sat down on his bed. It was impossible to say whether he liked the room or not. He pointed to my own bed with one hand.

'Here sleeps Ewald,' said my mother quickly, in English.

'No,' said Jasper. 'I need a room of my own!' Then he got up, waddled over to the window, and stared out at the building opposite.

We withdrew to the living room for a consultation. Once again, Peter advised us to send Jasper straight back. And I think Dad would have been glad to agree, but Mum wouldn't hear of it. 'We can't just give up!' she said. 'On his very first day, too! Just think what it would look like!'

Billie said it would be all right for me to sleep in her room, she wouldn't mind. Billie has a spare bed in her room for Granny, when Granny stays the night with us.

So I went back to my room and put everything I needed to sustain life into a laundry basket. Jasper was still standing at the window looking at the building opposite.

'Now you have your own room,' I told Jasper's back. I spoke in English, and I spoke in a friendly way, because I was so pleased I wouldn't have to share a room with him for the next six weeks.

Monday, 20th July

Billie and I slept late, because we'd stayed awake a long time the night before. It can be fun sharing a room with somebody you like. Billie and I discussed Life, and it was half-past two before we finally said goodnight to each other. We discussed Jasper too, and we didn't agree about him. Billie said she didn't think he was so bad at all. She said I'd simply swallowed Peter Stollinka's prejudices whole. You can't form a real opinion of someone after only half a day, she said, and so long as you can't form a real opinion you ought to think well of them. That sounded very high-minded, but I had a sort of feeling Billie was only standing up for Jasper because he behaved in ways our parents don't like. It struck me that she was delighted to find Mum and Dad had no idea how to cope with him. You can't go snapping at somebody else's child as if he were your own. And Jasper was not very promising audience material for lectures either, because he wouldn't admit to knowing any German. Not even my father could claim to be good enough at English to deliver lectures on good behaviour in that language.

So Billie and I didn't get up until nine-thirty. Mum looked at us rather sourly. She doesn't like people to 'lie in bed till all hours', as she puts it. Not even in the holidays. She's a natural early riser herself, and she wants us to be the same.

Mum told us Jasper was still asleep. We could tell that, because of the loud snores coming from my room. Mum said she'd really meant to show Jasper some of the sights of Vienna today: the Vienna Woods and the Kahlenberg and the Leopoldsberg, and Dad had left her the car on purpose. 'But if he sleeps much longer,' she said fretfully, looking at the clock, 'there won't be time.'

'Wake him up, then,' Billie suggested.

'Shall I?' Mum hesitated. Then she said, 'No, I'll let him have his sleep out on his first day here!'

Billie dug me in the ribs with her elbow. 'She daren't, that's what it is!' she said, giggling. 'Isn't that priceless? She *daren't* wake that boy up! I could give him five schillings for that!' (In the usual way my mother's an expert waker-up of people. You might almost think she enjoys it. Especially when she sets about you with a wet flannel, or pulls back the bedclothes.)

Jasper emerged from my room while we were having lunch. He staggered drowsily into the hall. We'd been watching out for him through the open door of the living room. The egg dumpling my mother was lifting to her mouth fell off her fork, and she let out a little squeal. Because Jasper was staggering about the hall naked! We don't usually go about naked in our family. There's no actual rule against it, but all the same we don't do it. (Except for Billie, who sometimes goes from her room to the bathroom in nothing but her knickers, but if I happen

51

to meet her I look away at once.)

Jasper staggered over to the larder and opened the larder door. When he saw the shelves of jam jars he shut the door again.

'It's the door on the left!' Billie told him, shouting in English. Out in the hall, Jasper staggered to the left, and went into the lavatory.

'Get him your dressing gown,' Mum told me.

'Why mine?' I protested. I'm not selfish, but my dressing gown is a very important item of my wardrobe, specially in the holidays.

'All right, then, get him mine,' said Mum.

'Why a dressing gown anyway?' asked Billie, with something ominous in her voice. 'Do you think naked people look disgusting or something?'

'Of course I don't,' said Mum.

'Then why shouldn't he be naked? I mean, it's not cold.' Billie was looking innocent as a lamb.

'Because we don't go about naked, and that's my last word,' said Mum, but Mum's last word doesn't have anything like the same effect on Billie as Dad's last word.

'We don't *have* to go about naked, no,' said Billie, 'but the question is, *may* he go about naked?'

'Oh, so you think Jasper looks nice naked?' Mum seemed to want to shift her ground in this argument.

'He wouldn't look any nicer in a pair of underpants,' said Billie.

I wanted to stand by her, out of fraternal solidarity, so I said, 'Anyway, there's nothing to see—his stomach's hanging down all over everything!'

Billie giggled, and Mum actually went red in the face, I swear she did.

We heard the lavatory being flushed.

'Ewald!' There was a note of panic in my mother's voice. 'Ewald, please get my dressing gown!'

But before I could do more than start to rise from my chair, Jasper had gone back into my room, i.e. his room. Billie grinned.

'Put my dressing gown on his bed,' Mum told me, 'and then I'm sure he'll realize he's meant to wear it!'

Billie gave me a look that said: Don't go! Don't take that dressing gown in there!

'Mum,' I said, 'your dressing gown has three rows of frills and a pattern of bunches of violets all over it! He'd never guess he was meant to wear that!'

'Then take him Dad's,' said Mum.

'He'll fall over and break his leg in Dad's,' said Billie. (Dad is nearly two metres tall.)

Jasper put an end to any more argument by coming out of my room, i.e. his room, again. This time he was wearing a T-shirt and a pair of baggy striped cotton underpants. He went into the kitchen without so much as glancing at us. We heard the fridge door open and shut, and then Jasper came back with a litre carton of milk, crossed the hall with the open milk carton raised to his lips, and disappeared back into my room, i.e. his room, leaving a wide trail of drops of milk behind him, because drinking milk straight from the carton is not easy.

'I've never seen anything like it in my life,' said Mum.

'We live and learn, don't we?' said Billie, getting up from the table. She was looking extremely pleased with herself.

Jasper came out to get more milk three times that day, and then our supply of milk cartons ran out. And he went to the lavatory three times. He never came out of the bedroom at all except to get milk or go to the lavatory. (I've decided to give up my claim to that room for the rest of this story. I'll just call it his room from now on.)

Jasper didn't turn up for supper either. 'He isn't hungry,' Billie told us, after she'd been sent to tell him it was supper-time.

But some time late that night, long after Billie and I had gone to bed, and Mum and Dad were in bed too, I heard footsteps in the hall. However, the light was not switched on. I'd have seen if it was, because Billie's bedroom door doesn't shut properly, so there's a streak of light underneath it when the hall light is on.

'He's prowling around the hall,' I told Billie, but she was already asleep. I pulled the bedclothes up and thought: well, that's what comes of asking a foreign child to stay! Now let them find out how to cope with him!

But this thought didn't really make me very happy. Somehow there'd been a very sad sound about those footsteps in the hall.

Tuesday, 21st July

Jasper slept until mid-day again, then drank two litres of milk and went back to his room.

'Things can't go on like this,' said my mother. She was obviously jittery.

Early that evening Mr and Mrs Pearson rang up. My father wasn't home yet. My mother had just gone out to the dairy, because we'd run out of milk again. Jasper had drunk it all.

When the Pearsons rang I answered the phone. But I

couldn't understand a thing, except that they were speaking from London and wanted to know how their son was. So I called Billie and handed her the phone. Billie took it and listened. (While she was listening, she covered the speaking end of the receiver with one hand and told me, 'They think I'm Mum again!' She was obviously pleased by this.) Then Billie spoke into the receiver. She said, 'Oh no, oh no!' once or twice, and, 'Really not!' And then, 'No, no, he is a nice boy, I like him!' Then she listened again, and after that she called through the door of Jasper's room, 'Your parents, Jasper!'

Jasper came out of his room in his baggy underpants. Billie handed him the receiver. Jasper took it, listened, shook his head, and handed it back to Billie. There was nothing but a lot of crackling, quacking sounds on the line. Our connection with London must have been broken.

'Sorry,' said Billie. Jasper nodded to her and went back to his room.

Just as he disappeared through the door, Mum came in, panting, with four cartons of milk. (We all arrive home panting, because of the four floors and the spiral staircase. Spiral staircases seduce you into taking them very fast.)

'The Pearsons rang again,' Billie told Mum.

'What did they say?' asked Mum, taking the milk into the kitchen. Billie followed her. So did I. Billie shut the kitchen door. 'So that he can't hear us,' she said. 'I think he can really understand German quite well.' Then Billie told us what the Pearsons had said, so far as she could understand it.

The Pearsons had asked if we were getting along with

Jasper all right, and if not we were to send him back. Because, as they knew themselves, he was a problem child. A difficult case. And they'd never have sent him off on a foreign exchange but for Tom's leg being in plaster. 'Although his psychiatrist says—' said Billie, but she didn't finish her sentence, because Mum interrupted her. 'His *what*?' asked Mum, looking horrified.

Billie shrugged her shoulders. 'Apparently he has a psychiatrist. And the Pearsons said the psychiatrist has been saying for some time it might be a good idea to send Jasper somewhere new, and different surroundings might help. Or something like that.'

'But why does he have a psychiatrist?' asked Mum, sitting down on the kitchen stool with the milk cartons on her lap.

Billie said she didn't know. Anyway, what she had just told us was mostly what she *thought* the Pearsons had meant. Her English wasn't up to diplomatic interpreters' standards, and she couldn't swear to the truth of every word. However, Billie added, the Pearsons were going to ring again tomorrow or the next day, in the evening, and Mum could find out more then.

We had boiled beef with chive sauce and potato purée for supper. Billie knocked on Jasper's door, and he came out and sat down with us. You could see my mother was glad of that. So was my father. He smiled at Mum. As much as to say: You see, we're getting somewhere, slowly but surely—patience does the trick!

Jasper sat down. He looked at the serving dish of food very suspiciously. My mother picked up his plate and gave him a large helping. I was watching Jasper, and I saw that now he was looking not only suspicious but cross

56

as well. You could tell from the corners of his mouth. I sympathized! *I* never like it when my mother picks up my own plate to serve me. It's not as if I were still a baby—I could help myself to what I want! But my mother doesn't believe I'd take the right amount of everything. I might help myself to too much meat and too few vegetables. Or too much sauce and not enough potatoes. Or just too much of everything! Or then again, too little of everything! My mother even serves out my father's food for him, as if *he* weren't old enough to know what's good for him either.

Jasper took his plate back. Then he stood up and fetched the bottle of tomato ketchup that was standing on the sideboard. We only have tomato ketchup with grilled meat. It doesn't go at all well with boiled beef and chive sauce! Still, you ought to let other people have what they like, and I didn't think Mum should have said, in horrified tones, 'No, Jasper, no, no, no!'

But anyway Jasper took no notice. He unscrewed the bottle and tipped its entire contents over his meat, potatoes and sauce. There was a large red mound on his plate now. Jasper picked up a spoon and ate the ketchup off the top of this mound until the beef, potatoes and sauce, now stained red, came back into view. Then he put down his spoon, picked up Dad's half-empty beer bottle, poured the beer still in the bottle into his glass, drank it, belched, got up and went back to his room.

Tears rose to my mother's eyes. She wiped them away, trying to smile. 'It's just my nerves!' she said. 'Just my stupid nerves!'

The situation didn't change. Jasper drank milk by the litre, and on Wednesday he ate the new bottle of ketchup Mum had bought. (After that she didn't buy any more.)

He stayed in his room. It was only at night that he came out and went groping around the hall in the dark. And on Thursday night I found out what he was doing there! Because when I heard him groping around again, I got up and went to the door, opened it just a crack, and peered out. It was dark in the hall, but the larder door was open, and the light was switched on in the larder.

Jasper was standing there getting a jar of apricot jam and a can of fish off the shelves. And he took a family pack of ice cream out of the freezer. Then he switched off the larder light and groped his way back to his room in the dark. He passed me so close I could have put out my hand and touched him, and I felt like whispering, 'That lot will make you feel sick!'

But I didn't. I thought he might be startled, and drop the jam jar.

Next morning I told Billie what I'd seen in the night. She made me swear solemnly not to tell Mum. I hadn't been going to, anyway. Not so much because I liked Jasper as because it would have made Mum even more nervous, and she was nothing but a bundle of nerves already. Dad was aware of that too. I heard him tell her one evening, 'You're all on edge, my dear! You'll never be able to stand having that boy around for six whole weeks! When the Pearsons ring again I'm going to tell them we simply can't cope with their son, and we'll have to send him back!' And then Dad said something cross about 'those people', and how it was an 'imposition, letting a child like that loose on perfect strangers'.

'If they're bringing him up to be such a little savage,' he added, 'they ought to shoulder the consequences themselves!'

And then Dad said, 'Well, at least it makes you appreciate your own children when you see what other kids can be like!'

This remark filled me with great satisfaction!

Saturday, 25th July

The day was a total disaster, beginning in the morning. Dad doesn't go to the office on Saturdays, and he always wants to 'make the most' of the day. That means going swimming, or for an expedition somewhere, or sometimes going to Granny's allotment. He gets up just as early on Saturdays as weekdays, and wanders around the apartment singing and making breakfast. He says he sings because he's feeling cheerful, but Billie says he sings to wake us up. Because he wants us to 'make the most of the day' with him too. But anyway, you can't go on sleeping with Dad bellowing out a song about La Paloma, and he's got me and Billie sitting down to breakfast by eight at the latest. (Mum's always the first up anyway.)

It was no different this Saturday, which was a fine, sunny day. 'We're going out,' said Dad, eating his roll. 'We'll show Jasper round, and eat out somewhere pleasant.'

'Why don't we go swimming?' Billie grumbled. 'It's

going to be boiling hot today.'

'Because we're going to show Jasper the Gürtel, that's why not,' said Dad. 'You can find swimming baths in big cities all over the world, but only Vienna has so many green open spaces around it as we have in the Gürtel.'

'I shouldn't think Jasper cares a bit about our green open spaces,' I said, but Dad just ignored me. He was telling Mum, in detail, which way he intended to drive, and the places where we might stop. Mum said miserably, 'Really, when I think of that boy munching peanuts in our car and spitting out the shells, I can't look forward to it at all. And I certainly don't want to go into any restaurant with that—that ketchup addict! I'd feel so ashamed!'

'He won't act like that today,' said Dad, confidently.

'Why not?' asked Mum.

'Because I'm here!' said Dad. That hurt Mum's feelings. 'Oh,' she said. 'You mean to say it's all my fault he's been behaving the way he has?'

Dad assured her he had not meant to say any such thing. However, he explained, he had been thinking things over. Since Mum didn't feel able to send Jasper back, because that would have been so awkward, we must try a new approach. Dad said that boy needed 'a firm hand'. He needed to sense that someone was in authority. And Dad said he was more gifted than Mum in that line.

'The best of luck,' said Mum, listlessly.

'Luck? It's not a matter of luck,' replied Dad. 'It's a matter of determination! He must learn that he has to adapt. Once he's adapted he'll realize he's better off that way! Children must be led until they know the right way to go!'

'For ever and ever, amen,' said Billie, and Dad flew into a temper.

'If you're too stupid to follow me,' he said, 'just hold your tongue. I can do without your immature comments!'

'But I can't,' said Billie, and then Dad threatened to slap her. Her face went red, but she said no more.

'We're starting at nine,' Dad told me. 'Just you remember that!' When Dad's angry with Billie he takes it out on me too, which is a nasty trick. Not so much because it's unfair as because of Billie herself. I don't mind now I've seen through it, but it used to be a very nasty trick. It worked like this: Billie would annoy Dad, and he'd be cross with her. And cross with me too. And then *I* was furious with Billie because I thought it was her fault Dad was being horrible to me. Then I'd be horrible to Billie myself, when she hadn't done anything at all to me! I don't think Dad plans it like this. He just gets cross, and some of his crossness rubs off on everyone else. But Billie says, and I must admit I think she's right, that if something turns out nasty then it *is* nasty, whether it was meant to be nasty or not.

Dad had another roll and butter and honey, and swallowed his bad temper along with it. When he'd finished the roll he said to Billie, quite nicely, 'Go and wake Jasper up!'

But Billie had not yet swallowed her own annoyance. 'Why does it always have to be me?' she asked. She shook her head and went on eating. I went to the lavatory so as not to be caught between the pair of them. I knew that if I stayed at the breakfast table Dad would tell *me* to go and wake Jasper up. Then Billie would give me a look saying:

61

Don't you dare. And Dad would give me a look saying: Run along like a good boy. I was safe from either in the lavatory. I sat there, not doing anything, just waiting. Until I heard Mum's voice saying, 'Very well then, if my lady here won't go, *I'll* go and wake him up!'

I'd better be there, I thought, coming out of the lavatory and hurrying after Mum. Because I'd stolen a look inside Jasper's room once or twice, when he was on his way to get milk or go to the lavatory, and I knew only too well that Mum would throw a fit at the sight of what I'd seen in there. She did overdo it a bit, though, starting to sob and almost fainting when she opened the door. I mean, it wasn't in such an appalling mess as all that. All Jasper's clothes were lying about the floor. And he'd taken my electric trains out of the orange boxes, along with all the rails and the papier mâché hills and so on that went with the set, and there were empty jam jars and sardine cans and ice cream packs lying about too, of course. And a lot of used tissues. And there were a great many flies in the room, which was not surprising, because you get a great many flies in summer anyway, and they like to congregate where they can find sticky, greasy, messy, gooey paper wrappings, and cans with fishy oil in them, and dirty jam jars.

Actually, the only really revolting thing was the fishy oil that had got spilt on the floor and Jasper's scattered clothes. Jasper had dumped the empty cans on the floor, and he must have tripped over them. But you can always wash clothes, and the floor of that room is vinyl, so no irreversible disaster had happened.

Mum sobbed so loud that Billie and Dad came running along, and Jasper woke up. Startled, Jasper jumped out of bed, looking round in a baffled way. He stood there in front of us, naked but for a pair of red socks and (I swear this is true) a wide leather belt round his waist. There was a kind of sheath with a knife in it fastened to the belt. (Over the next few weeks I found out a lot about Jasper, but to this day I don't know why he slept with a knife at his waist.)

Mum went on sobbing. I ought to explain that my mother is a very tidy woman. In fact Grandmother says she's neurotic about it. Mum chases every least little bit of dirt as if she were the Devil himself chasing souls. When she sees some fluff under a cupboard, she gets out the vacuum cleaner, and she doesn't just hoover up the fluff, she goes through the whole apartment. And say she comes into my room and sees my shoes on the floor by the bed, not tidily side by side but at an angle, she'll go over and put them straight. She doesn't notice she's doing this. It's just her subconscious at work, making her straighten things out. The mats on the table, my writing things on my desk. She changes the beds once a week and washes the curtains once a fortnight. If I'm helping her in the kitchen, and I use the cloth for wiping glasses instead of the one for wiping china or the one for wiping pots and pans, she gets annoyed and washes and dries everything all over again.

So you can see what a shock the sight of Jasper's room gave my mother. My father was shocked too, but that was by the sight of Jasper himself.

'He's filthy dirty too,' said Dad. He was right. Jasper was covered by a positive coating of grime. I suddenly realized that ever since Jasper came to stay with us (and by now he'd been with us six days) he hadn't once been

63

into the bathroom.

Suddenly a grim and determined expression came over my father's face, and he grabbed Jasper's shoulder. 'Come on!' he said, in English.

Jasper struggled and clung to the door frame, but my father is very strong. He dragged Jasper away from the door, through the hall and into the bathroom. Then he closed the bathroom door.

When Dad was in the bathroom with Jasper, Mum stopped sobbing and went to fetch the laundry basket, the vacuum cleaner and the rubbish bucket. As if she had to halt an epidemic in its tracks, she swept all Jasper's scattered clothes into the basket, threw the cans, ice cream wrappings, tissues and even, to my surprise, the empty jam jars into the rubbish bucket, and started hoovering like mad. Panting as she did so. While she worked, she kept giving orders. 'Billie, get me a bucket of water!' and, 'Billie, fetch me a duster!' and, 'Billie, bring me the floor-cloth!' (I brought the floor-cloth, because I really don't see why Mum should land Billie, as her only child of the feminine gender, with all the housework jobs like that.)

The vacuum cleaner was humming loudly, Mum was giving orders even louder, but loudest of all were the yells coming from the bathroom. Jasper was roaring his head off!

'He'll murder him,' I told Mum.

Breathing hard as she hoovered away, Mum said, 'No, Dad won't hurt him, he's only washing him!' (I decided not to explain it wasn't Jasper I'd been worried about; I was thinking of the knife he wore round his waist, and the chances of his using it in self-defence.)

64

It was about half an hour before Mum had the filthy bedroom back to its usual state of painful cleanliness, and I'd put my trains and railway back in their proper places in the orange boxes. Towards the end of that half-hour the roars from the bathroom stopped, and when we'd finished with Jasper's room Dad emerged, looking exhausted but satisfied.

'I emptied a bottle of shampoo over his head,' he said, 'and I soaped him from head to foot, and gave him hot and cold showers. That dirt must have built up on him over the years! I had to use pumice stone on the soles of his feet.'

Mum looked at the time. 'Nearly nine,' she said.

Dad pointed to the bathroom and said, 'Give him a few minutes to get his breath back. Then I'll fetch him out to get dressed.'

Mum went over to my bed, where she'd laid out the few items of Jasper's clothing she hadn't thought needed washing. She looked at them, frowning. Apparently she didn't like them. 'Billie,' she said, 'get me your big white sweater. That ought to fit him. And a pair of those huge socks Grandmother gave you!'

I hadn't been taking much notice of Billie until this point, but now I looked at her. She was standing by the window, crimson in the face and quivering with rage. When Billie gets into that state she can be terrifying.

'Go and fetch them, then!' said Mum. Billie didn't move, and Mum misunderstood. 'Don't be so mean!' she said. 'You've got a dozen sweaters, you can easily lend him one! I'm not going out with him in those scruffy clothes, and Dad's things would be too big for him!'

Here we go, I thought, watching Billie, and I was right.

65

Billie clenched her shaking fists, stamped her foot, and shouted, 'Oh, how I hate you! Can't you leave anyone in peace? Do you have to force *everyone* to be the way you want? You might at least leave poor Jasper alone! You and Dad, you're so square and bourgeois it just isn't true!'

After shouting this, she turned to run out of the room, but Dad caught her and slapped her face, twice. Billie took it like a queen! She didn't try to cover her face with her arms, she didn't bat an eyelash. She even looked as if she were ready for a third slap, but when it didn't come she stalked into her room, head held high.

'She's staying at home, and that's my last word!' said Dad. As if *that* would be any kind of punishment in the circumstances.

Mum was looking angrily at Dad, and if I hadn't been there she'd probably have given him a lecture. Mum's against slapping people. She says you only ought to slap small children who can't understand words yet. (Billie thinks it's even worse to slap small children than large ones, because really small kids haven't the faintest idea why it's happening, and they get terribly frightened. However, nobody knows, because they can't say so!)

'Right,' said Dad, rubbing his hands, which seemed to be hurting him after he'd slapped Billie's face. 'Well, now I'll get that boy out of there!' He went to the bathroom and tried to open the door, but it was locked on the inside. Dad hammered on the door. 'Open the door, Jasper, and let me in!' he shouted in English, about a dozen times. Nothing moved inside the bathroom.

'He's more likely to listen to Billie,' said Mum, very flustered. 'She'll have to get him out!' She went to Billie's bedroom door, tried the handle, rattled it, and then shouted, 'Open the door, Billie, and let me in!'

It was a daft situation! Two white doors with a parent shaking the door-handle of each, demanding to be let in!

Dad was the first to give it up as hopeless. 'Fine!' he said bitterly. 'They can just stay in there! We're off!'

I didn't dare object. Mum fetched her handbag and put her blue straw hat on. Dad got his jacket. Then he took Billie's key-ring, which was hanging on a hook in the hall, and put it in his pocket. And he got the spare front-door key out of the drawer in the hall cupboard. 'They're not going to leave this apartment!' he said, very nastily.

And we left. Dad locked the door twice from the outside, double-locking both the top lock and the lower one, which we usually lock only when we're going away on holiday.

So I spent that Saturday seeing the sights of the Gürtel in my own native city of Vienna, and Dad told me all the stuff he'd been going to tell Jasper, only in German. Which was rather a pity, because I'd been quite looking forward to hearing what Dad had to say about the sights of Vienna in English!

Sunday, 26th July

It was eight when Billie and I woke up. Mum woke us, coming into our room and opening the window. 'You want some fresh air in here,' she said. Then she went out again. Billie pulled the bedclothes up over her head. I remembered that she'd been going to tell me something important in bed yesterday evening. 'But not until *they've* gone to bed too,' she had said. 'You never know, they might be listening at the door!' Unfortunately, I'd gone to sleep. Dad's sight-seeing tour of the green open spaces of Vienna had worn me out. All that oxygen and all those miles of driving are very tiring.

'Billie!' I said.

Billie's head emerged from under her bedclothes.

'You were going to tell me something last night,' I said. 'Something important.'

'Yes, but you went to sleep first,' said Billie. She sat up in bed, and was about to begin telling me when Mum came back into the room, this time with clean sheets.

'Come on, up you get!' she said. 'I want to change the beds.'

'Later,' said Billie. She was speaking to me, and she meant she'd tell me the important thing later, but Mum thought she meant changing the sheets. 'No, now!' she said. 'Later we're going to Schönbrunn to see the Palace.'

Sighing, we hauled ourselves out of bed and left the room. The door of Jasper's room was open, and everything was spick and span inside. My mother must have been in there already, nipping any threat of untidiness in the bud. Jasper wasn't in the room. He was sitting in the living room having breakfast. His hair was wet; obviously Dad had washed him yet again. Jasper looked as if his spirit was broken, rather like the mentally disturbed gorilla in the zoo.

Dad was having his breakfast too. He gave us a brief nod. I think he wasn't quite sure whether he was on speaking terms with Billie again or not: whether the two slaps wiped out her calling him square and bourgeois, or whether he had to punish her further by taking no notice of her for the whole day.

I ate my breakfast, and I noticed Billie and Jasper exchanging a couple of glances. Sad, meaning glances. I tried to join in this exchange of glances too, and I managed to meet Billie's eyes, but Jasper looked straight past me.

Then Dad announced the programme. 'We start off at nine,' he said. 'We're going to see Schönbrunn Palace.'

'I'm not,' said Billie. 'I feel sick.'

'You feel sick, do you?' said Dad angrily. 'Well, if that's how you want it, we can do very well without you!'

Billie got up. I saw her give Jasper an encouraging look. Jasper nodded, very slightly, and then, in English, he too said, 'I feel sick!' And he got up as well. Billie marched out of the living room, and Jasper followed her. I felt very lonely. Jealous, too, because I realized something must have been going on between Jasper and Billie. Something I didn't know about, because I'd been dragged off to see the green open spaces. If I hadn't known that Billie's only interested in handsome men of eighteen or over, I'd have thought the pair of them had fallen in love or something.

Well, I didn't want to be left out for another whole day, so I said, with the courage of despair, '*I* feel sick too!' and dashed out of the living room. I went to Billie's room, and on the way I passed Jasper's open door. Jasper was lying fully clothed on the bed, as if he were in his coffin, his eyes closed, his hands folded over his stomach. I found Billie in the same position in her room, lying on her freshly made bed. So I lay down on the spare bed as if I were in *my* coffin, and closed my own eyes.

'You on strike too?' asked Billie softly.

'Sure!' I said.

Billie sighed. 'Do you think,' she said, 'Mum and Dad

69

will go off to see Schönbrunn Palace on their own?'

'I shouldn't think so,' I said.

'I wish I could stop up my ears with my headphones again!' said Billie.

'Well, why don't you?' I said.

'Can't,' said Billie. 'Then Jasper wouldn't have anyone. *You* don't like him either.'

I muttered something defensive.

'No, you don't,' said Billie. 'You don't like him because they landed you with him without asking you first!'

'It was Tom they wanted—' I began, but Billie interrupted me.

'Well, thank goodness the sainted Tom didn't come!'

'What do you mean?' I said. 'You liked his photograph!'

'People can make mistakes, can't they?' said Billie. 'Get Jasper to tell you what he's like!'

The idea of my getting Jasper to tell me anything struck me as absurd, and I was angry with Billie. 'Oh, wrap your precious Jasper up in tissue paper, with a pretty ribbon on the top!' I spat.

'Well, of course, when Mummy and Daddy don't like someone little Diddums mustn't like him either!' Billie spat back. She sat up. 'So why are you lying there, then? Why don't you go and see Schönbrunn like a good boy? I expect they'll buy you an ice afterwards.'

'You're being foul,' I said.

'Yes,' said Billie, and then, after a short pause, 'Sorry, Waldi.'

She got up, slipped out into the hall, and came back grinning. 'I think they're going,' she whispered. 'Dad told Mum he'd put his old trousers on, and Mum said she'd make sandwiches!'

Billie was right. We heard rapid footsteps in the hall, and Mum said something about taking a basket in case the blackcurrants were ripe. Then we heard Mum ringing Granny up. 'We're going to the allotment,' she said. 'Would you like to come?' And then, 'No, the children don't want to go. They don't feel like it.'

'Typical!' muttered Billie. 'Just so long as nobody notices what goes on in this place!' She imitated Mum's voice. 'The children don't want to go, they don't feel like it. Ha, ha! We lock them up, we knock them about a bit, but apart from that we have such a happy, harmonious family life!'

She was right, but all the same I didn't like hearing all the rage and hatred in her voice. I mean, our parents are the only ones we have. We can't turn them in for a different model. And apart from their bad points, the ones that annoy Billie so much, they have a number of good points too. But I didn't think this was the right moment to say so to her.

When the front door was locked from outside, Billie went to the window.

'He's double-locking it,' I said. 'Double-locking both locks.'

'Who cares?' said Billie. She was watching the street below. 'I'm going to wait until they've got into the car and driven off,' she said, 'and then I'm going to the Prater with Jasper. Want to come? We went yesterday too. Jasper likes the Prater!'

This is crazy, I thought. How's she going to get out of the double-locked door, when Dad's got all the keys with him? How can she have got out yesterday?

71

'It's just a matter of using one's head, Waldi,' said Billie. 'Surely he can't expect me to put up with this kind of thing, at the age of fifteen? Where exactly *are* we? In jail? Back in the Middle Ages?' Billie laughed, in a nasty way. 'Good, there they go,' she said. She left her observation post and went into the hall.

'Parents gone?' asked Jasper from his room, in English.

Billie called, 'Parents gone! Waldi will come with us!' She was speaking English too.

Jasper came out of his room. He was wearing Billie's big sweater and a pair of scruffy jeans, with his wide leather belt over the sweater. There was a small purse hanging from it as well as the knife in its sheath.

Billie went over to the telephone, lifted the receiver and dialled. I heard the bell ring once at the other end of the line, and then someone said, 'Hullo,' loud enough for me to hear it too. Billie spoke down the phone. 'It's Sybille Mittermeier,' she said. 'Would you mind coming up again, Mr Prowaznik?' And then, 'Thank you, that's really kind of you!' She put the receiver down again. Now I saw it all! Mr Prowaznik is our old caretaker, and he has spare keys to the apartment, in case there's a fire or a burst pipe while we're out.

A minute or so later Mr Prowaznik had unlocked the door. We left the apartment, and Mr Prowaznik locked up again after us.

'We'll be back at five at the latest,' said Billie.

'Suppose your parents get back first?' Mr Prowaznik sounded rather worried.

'They won't,' I said.

'Ah well,' sighed Mr Prowaznik, and then he chuckled. 'Who cares if they do?' he said. 'Locking up children, whoever heard of such a thing? Wouldn't do that to my Wotan!' (Wotan is Mr Prowaznik's dog.)

We ran down the spiral staircase, with Mr Prowaznik waving goodbye.

We took a tram to the Prater, where there's a big amusement park. We played the fruit machines for ages, and Jasper kept winning. We ate very garlicky sausages, and Jasper had a fried herring on a stick with crispy peanut twirls. He said this combination was almost as good as fish and chips, which was his main source of nourishment at home. What's more, Jasper told us this in German, with just a few English words mixed in. And he smiled at me once that day. When I felt a bit sick riding on the big dipper, and he smiled and said I'd soon feel better.

Billie was paying for us to have goes on things at the Prater, with the money she got for her good report. 'The Prater's more fun than CDs,' she said. She usually spends almost all her money on CDs.

We weren't home till a few minutes after six, because there was one particular machine from which Jasper could hardly tear himself away. But we could easily have left it even later. We'd been back in the apartment for over an hour, with the door re-locked after us by Mr Prowaznik, when Mum and Dad came home. They had two baskets full of blackcurrants, and Mum told Billie to come into the kitchen and pick them over. I helped her. Jasper came into the kitchen and helped too. In tones of heavy sarcasm, Mum asked if we were still feeling sick, and would we like her to make us some bread and milk? Just the thing for sensitive young stomachs. We said no. 'I'm not hungry, thanks,' said Billie. So did I, and Jasper nodded. This annoyed Mum. She'd obviously been expecting us to beg for ham sandwiches, or something like that. After all, so far as she knew we hadn't had any lunch.

Then Billie belched, three times, bringing up a powerful smell of garlic. So powerful that the whole kitchen smelt of it. This annoyed Mum even more. We never have garlic at home, because Mum doesn't like it. And then she saw the three red paper roses on the hall cupboard. Jasper had got them at the shooting range and given them to Billie.

'Where did those roses come from?' asked Mum, looking at us in surprise. Red paper roses are not the kind of thing we usually bring home. Jasper grinned. Billie shrugged her shoulders. Mum looked suspicious. I feel awkward in that sort of situation, so I said quickly, 'They were in my desk. I cleared it out today!'

Mum accepted this, but Billie shook her head, and whispered to me, 'Why did you say that? It would have given her something to think about!'

Monday, 27th July

Dad had to go to the office again, so we had a peaceful day. Jasper didn't have to wash or come in to breakfast. He did have to let Mum into his room to clean it, and there was a small clash with her when she picked up several of Jasper's stones which were lying on the floor and put them into a carton. That made Jasper growl again, so savagely that Mum's feelings were hurt, and she took the vacuum cleaner and left the room.

Mum was not on good terms with me and Billie either. I think she didn't really like to see us getting on all right with Jasper. She probably thought of him as exactly the kind of child who'd be a bad influence. She'd had a holy terror of such children ever since Billie and I were born. (When I was at primary school, for instance, she used to come and see the teacher every term asking her to put me at another desk, because the boy sitting next to me was a bad influence on me. Thank goodness the teacher never did.)

Mum didn't like it when we spent the afternoon playing cards, either. Mum thinks playing cards is a vice. Actually, you can see her point. Her father, who's been dead for years, was the sort who's always playing cards. For money, too. But he hardly ever won anything. Once he spent his whole week's wages gambling on a Friday night. But Billie and Jasper and I were only playing for old buttons—I mean, there *is* a difference! However, Mum didn't see it, and when I told her how good Jasper was at Racing Demon, she said sourly, 'I might have known it!' And she added, 'Does he smoke too?' I shook my head, although I didn't really know.

Then, late that evening, when I had to go to the lavatory and I was passing my parents' bedroom door on the way, I heard Mum and Dad talking. I'd caught the word 'Jasper', so I stopped to listen. (I'm not ashamed to say so. Most people do listen at doors and read other people's letters, and some of them even look through keyholes. They just won't admit it.)

This is what I overheard:

Dad (impatiently): Look, you're going round in circles! You don't want him here, but you say we can't send him back! That's nonsense! You *must* do one or the other!

Mum (bitterly): Well, now you've told Mr Pearson on the phone that we're getting on all right with him—

Dad (interrupting Mum): That was just an ordinary polite white lie—

Mum (interrupting Dad):—we can hardly ring up again two days later and say we can't stand him.

Dad: It's all very well for you to talk! I couldn't tell the man over the phone what a little savage his son is. I did drop a hint.

Mum (scornfully): A hint! Well, if he didn't get the hint, you weren't dropping it hard enough!

Dad: What *do* you want, then? You say we can't keep him here. You also say we can't send him back. Do you want me to murder him, or what?

Mum (horrified): For goodness' sake! Don't say such things, even in jest! (Short pause.) I think we must go slowly. A week or ten days of it . . . I expect I can stand that. (Firmly.) But I'm not taking him away on holiday with us, I won't have that! It would be no sort of rest at all! (Another short pause.) We'll keep him here for the time being, and a few days before we go away we'll ring up and say—well, we'll make some sort of excuse. We could say your mother's dying—

Dad (annoyed): Why mine? Let's say *your* mother's dying!

Mum: All right, mine! It doesn't make any difference. Are you superstitious or something?

Dad: No, I'm not. I just don't like saying people are ill.

Mum: Okay, then, we must think of something else. For instance, we have to go abroad on urgent business . . . (Short pause.) Why do people have to go abroad on urgent business? Any idea?

Dad (thoughtfully): Wait a minute ... er ... why? Because ... let me think! (Yawn.) I'm too tired now. (Confidently.) But I'll think of something! I'll ask Petermeier at the office tomorrow. He's an expert at thinking up excuses ...

At this point I needed to go to the lavatory so badly that I couldn't stay and overhear any more.

Tuesday, 28th July
Wednesday, 29th July
Thursday, 30th July
Friday, 31st July

Billie and I agreed not to tell Jasper about the conversation I'd overheard, because it must be horrible to be somewhere people don't want you.

In bed in the evenings, when Jasper couldn't hear us, we discussed ways of sabotaging the plan to get rid of him. But we couldn't think of a good one. We did agree, however, that we wanted Jasper to stay. And not just because he was a thorn in our parents' flesh. (At least, that wasn't my main reason.) I was getting to like Jasper a bit better every day. Of course he was very dirty and untidy, about his own body as well as other things. But he was okay. And when I knew him better, I could understand the things that had set me against him so much at first. For instance, he'd only insisted on having a room to himself because he snores so badly that people have been telling him all his life how awful it is to sleep with him. And he growls if you touch his collection of stones because his mother's tried throwing them away several times. They wouldn't let him have his stones in the boarding schools he's been to, either.

Jasper told us he'd been to four boarding schools, one term in each of them. Private boys' schools in England. They expelled him from two, and he ran away from the other two. And if they hadn't expelled him from the first two he'd have run away from those as well, because schools like that are horrible, Jasper said. Apparently the masters are pigs, and the older boys are even bigger pigs. And someone like Jasper, who isn't quite the same as other people, has a very bad time, especially when he's rather clumsy and no good at games.

We asked Jasper why he'd been sent to these places, then? 'My father wanted me to go,' he said.

'But why didn't he want your brother Tom to go to one too?' Billie asked.

'His father is not the same as my father,' said Jasper. We waited for him to tell us more, but he didn't seem to want to talk about it. We soon got the general idea, though: Jasper was just over fourteen, and Tom was only just thirteen. When Jasper was a tiny baby his mother had been divorced from Jasper's father, and she married somebody else and had Tom. That sort of thing happens quite a lot.

We went swimming with Jasper too. On our own, without Mum. He wasn't at all clumsy in the water, he could dive and swim like a fish, and stay in the water for ages.

And on Thursday we went to the Prater on our own again, with the money I got for *my* good report.

Billie and I kept Jasper's untidy habits from Mum as well as we could. We picked up his used tissues, we threw away the empty milk cartons, we even put his dirty underwear in the linen basket. (Jasper didn't notice any of this. He isn't untidy on purpose.) We hoped that would soften Mum's heart. Whether we succeeded I don't really know, but as there wasn't any reason for her to lose her temper with him now, she didn't. She just looked at him with a faintly martyred expression. He still didn't turn up for supper or lunch, and naturally she thought that was dreadful. At Friday suppertime she told Dad, 'We can't let things go on like this, if only for nutritional reasons! Milk may be very healthy, but milk on its own isn't enough!'

'Then unlock the larder again,' Billie suggested. 'So he can get what he likes!' (Since Mum had discovered that Jasper was helping himself from her store cupboard, she had kept the larder locked, and the key was on her key-ring.)

But Mum didn't think much of this self-service notion of Billie's. 'He's having the wrong sort of diet,' she said. 'Anyone can see that. If he ate properly he wouldn't be such a flabby monster!'

I pushed my plate away and stood up.

'Aren't you going to finish that?' asked Mum.

'No,' I said. 'I can't sit here and listen to you being so rude about my friend!' And I told Dad, 'You always wanted me to have a friend! Well, now I have, and I'm not letting you insult him!'

Billie looked approvingly at me.

'Does he mean that *Jasper* is his friend?' Mum asked Dad.

'That's what he means,' said Dad, rubbing his nose with one finger, which is a sign that he's thinking hard. I didn't want to disturb him while he was thinking. I left the living room and went to Jasper's room to play poker.

Saturday, 1st August

Dad got a stomach upset on Friday night and spent Saturday morning in bed, when he wasn't in the lavatory. Mum had a headache, which she thought was the first symptom of a similar stomach upset, though Dad kept telling her his hadn't started with a headache.

'It takes different people in different ways at the start,' said Mum, and to be on the safe side she drank camomile tea and ate rusks, and sent Billie to do the shopping. But Billie wanted to wash her hair and blow it dry, so she sent *me* to do the shopping. I didn't ask Jasper whether he wanted to come to the supermarket with me, because having Jasper with you in a supermarket is not a good idea. He takes things. Well, to be blunt, he steals them. Chewing gum and boiled sweets and chocolate, just about anything he fancies. He does it very cleverly. Billie and I never saw him taking anything in a shop, we only found out when he showed us in the street. He can't see that it's a stupid thing to do. He says that when the shopkeeper works out the price of his goods he's reckoning on having ten per cent stolen anyway, so if no one stole anything, says Jasper, he'd make even more profit. Shopkeepers don't lower their prices if nobody steals anything for a month. The trouble is, says Jasper, that it's always the same people who steal, so the people who never steal anything are paying for it. However, he says, he can't help it if some people are fanatically honest. That's Jasper all over.

I tried explaining that this sort of theory isn't the point, it's a bad idea in practice. I know, because of Ilona from my class. Ilona was always nicking things too, chewing gum and ballpoint pens and all sorts of other stuff, and everyone knew she was very clever at it, but she got caught all the same. The first time, her parents had to pay for what she took, she was in disgrace at home, and that was all. But the second time, the school and the social services heard all about it, and she spent ages at the police station. It must have been dreadful. And the people in our class who used to accept Ilona's chewing gum, and write with her stolen ballpoint pens, whispered about her behind her back, and Wolfgang Emberger said he reckoned Ilona had something to do with the stamps Herbert Pivonka lost, because after all, she was used to pinching things. Even though Wolfgang Emberger used to stuff his face with the things Ilona pinched—the edible ones, that is.

When I told Jasper this, he was quite impressed, and thought I might be about sixty per cent right, and when Billie added earnestly, 'Crime really doesn't pay!' he was ninety per cent impressed. But as far as I was concerned, the remaining ten per cent was more than enough of an uncertainty factor! You don't deliberately expose someone who's at risk to danger. I hated to think what would happen if Jasper was taken off to the police station over a few silly packets of chewing gum! He could have been prosecuted, because he was over fourteen and supposed to be answerable for his actions.

So I went to the supermarket on my own, and found Peter Stollinka there, pushing a trolley.

'Still got him?' Peter asked me.

'Of course,' I said, as if that was perfectly natural. Then I asked Peter, 'Listen, why don't you like him, anyway?'

It would be too boring and too much bother to write down everything Peter said and everything I said, word for word. However, after half an hour walking round the supermarket a great deal had become clear to me. In brief, the story went as follows:

Jasper's mother had got divorced from Jasper's father when Jasper was still an embryo inside her. (According to Peter, because his father was as much of a pig as Jasper!) Then, a year later, she married Mr Pearson. And Jasper's father married again too. He married somebody called Mary. Jasper's father suddenly decided that he wanted little Jasper. And Jasper's mother, who had just had Tom, agreed. So Jasper went to live with his father and Mary. Then, when he was eight or nine, Peter wasn't quite sure which, Jasper's father got divorced from Mary too, or maybe she got divorced from him, or they both got divorced from each other. And Mary wanted to keep Jasper, because she'd had him so long, and he was like her own child to her. But Jasper's mother wouldn't let her. She wanted Jasper back. They couldn't agree about it, so they went to court. And the judge decided that Mary couldn't have Jasper because she wasn't related to him. It was decided that Jasper should belong to his mother during the week and his father on Sundays and at holiday times. But Jasper didn't go along with this decision. As soon as he was left on his own even for a minute, whether it was a weekday or a Sunday, he ran away to Mary. Then Mary had to bring him back, because otherwise she'd have been kidnapping him. 'That's why he got sent away to those boarding schools,' Peter Stollinka told me. 'The people there have more time and more ways of stopping a person running away.'

I learned a lot more from Peter Stollinka too, of course, How Jasper once bit Tom so badly Tom had to go to the doctor. How he once locked himself in the lavatory and wouldn't come out all day, and the rest of the Pearson family had to use the next door neighbour's lavatory. How he threw the chess set his father had given him for Christmas out of the window as soon as he got it. The heavy wooden box only just missed hitting a passer-by on the head. And last summer he poured a plate of hot tomato soup over Peter Stollinka's head, and another time he kicked Peter's shin so hard it was 'almost' broken. And he often spat at Tom and pulled Tom's dark hair. And finally I learned that Jasper had stopped running away since the beginning of this year, because Mary had married again, and now she lived in America. 'He knows he can't swim the Atlantic to get to her,' said Peter. So Jasper wouldn't have to go to boarding school any more. 'Which is a pity,' said Peter, 'because now Tom's lumbered with him all the time. But when Tom wrote to me he said Jasper wasn't anything like so savage these days. He's stopped hitting people and yelling. He just sulks and stinks and eats himself silly!'

I lugged two shopping bags and three plastic carrier bags full of food home, and hauled them up the spiral staircase in two instalments.

Billie was still in the bathroom, blow-drying her long hair. Jasper was sitting on the floor in his room, sorting out his stones. (Not a day passed when he didn't spend some time sorting out his stones.)

I put my bags and carriers in the kitchen. Good, tidy boy that I am, I even put the perishable stuff in the fridge. Then I read the newspaper I'd brought home until I didn't hear the sound of the hair-dryer any more, and then I called, 'Billie!' Billie looked out of the bathroom to see what I wanted, and I beckoned to her and told her I had something to tell her, but I wanted to tell Mum and Dad too, so would she come into their bedroom with me, and then I wouldn't have to tell the same story twice.

So we went into their bedroom.

'Got my newspaper?' asked my bedridden father.

'Did you buy my camomile tea?' asked my busy mother. She was busy cleaning the mirrors. (There's a wardrobe with eight doors in their bedroom, and it has a mirror on each door. My mother spends half an hour every day polishing up those mirrors.)

I said I'd got the tea and the newspaper, but I had something important to tell them. And then I gave them Jasper's life story. I don't know if I described it in an especially touching way, but my mother was certainly especially touched. When I got to the bit where Mary didn't want to give Jasper back, Mum stopped polishing the mirrors. And when I got to Jasper being sent to boarding school she lit herself a cigarette, though she won't usually have any smoking in the bedroom. By the time I'd finished telling Jasper's story, I had a deeply moved mother smoking as she sat on the side of the bed occupied by a deeply moved father, also smoking, while Billie, who is sometimes very soft-hearted, was standing by the window wiping tears from her eyes.

'That's dreadful!' murmured my father. 'Imagine treating children like that! No wonder they turn out the

84

way they do! It's a marvel they don't kill themselves!'

Mum stubbed out her cigarette in the saucer of Dad's cup of camomile tea (if you knew her you'd know this was an inconceivable crime for her to commit), and stood up. Then she said, 'I'm sorry—I really *am* sorry!' and went out of the room with the ash-filled saucer. Dad was staring straight ahead, rubbing his nose.

Billie said, 'And all you two can think of is how to get rid of him fast! I think that's just marvellous, I really do!'

Dad looked startled. 'What? No—I mean, we weren't!' he stammered. How was he to know I'd been eavesdropping on their plan to send Jasper home?

Mum came back to the bedroom. 'I had no idea he'd had such a bad time!' she said.

'Well, you have now,' said Billie. And Mum nodded.

Sunday, 2nd August

Mum went to more trouble than I'd have thought possible! She unlocked the larder again, and told Billie to tell Jasper he could help himself whenever he liked. And when she met Jasper she smiled at him, rather timidly.

Dad rose from his sick-bed at mid-day. He said he was feeling better, and he asked if we'd like to go out anywhere. (N.B.: he didn't *say* where we were going, he asked our opinion!) He said to Jasper, in English, 'Have you a wish to forbring the day?' meaning was there something he'd like to do?

Jasper grinned slightly, and said, in very bad German, he'd like to go to the Prater. (He can speak German much better than he did, but he just wanted to answer Dad back in the same kind of language.)

85

And Dad really did take us to the Prater, and he actually played the fruit machines, quite enthusiastically. I believe he enjoyed it. Billie said she thought it was really rather touching, and I think she was right.

Monday, 3rd August
Tuesday, 4th August
Wednesday, 5th August
Thursday, 6th August
Friday, 7th August

Our apartment smelt funny because Mum was frying chips for Jasper four times a day. And she grilled him mackerel, herrings and even trout, as the best substitute she could provide for his favourite dish of fish and chips. Jasper ate and ate, and whenever he took a plateful he smiled broadly at Mum, and Mum smiled back. In fact they kept grinning at each other like a couple of painted rocking horses. They hadn't yet reached the point where they could talk to each other, though.

Dad brought English comics home for Jasper every evening, and Jasper sat up late at night reading them. Sometimes he read a book he'd brought with him instead. It was called *Finnegan's Wake*, by somebody called James Joyce. Jasper told us he didn't understand a word of it, but it was a terrific book all the same.

We all five played poker in the evenings. Mum turned out to be marvellous at poker—a real gambler. 'Just like your father,' said Dad, and Mum said, 'Yes, precisely! That's why I'm so against it!'

We watched the Friday night film on television too, and laughed a lot, because Dad kept dropping off to sleep and only woke up when people fired shots. Then he would mutter, 'All this violence!' and fall asleep again.

And Jasper had a bath that evening, before the Friday night film. Without being told to. Mum was very proud of that.

'Should I give him a word of praise?' she asked me. I thought that would be overdoing it. But I gave *her* a word of praise. I told her she'd been really great these last few days.

Mum was tremendously pleased. 'I'm not really a monster,' she said. 'When I *know* how someone comes to be so disturbed, I can understand him.'

Billie, who was listening, said reproachfully, 'That's just what gets me down about you! You'd never dream of simply liking a person without understanding him!'

I nudged Billie to get her to shut up, but she wouldn't. She went on, 'Your trouble is you're only prepared to love people if they behave perfectly! If they do you'll love them back in return. You don't really love Jasper at all! You feel sorry for him, but love's quite different! You wouldn't love *us*, either, if we didn't do any work at school, and we smoked hash and stole money!'

The longer Billie went on, the paler and more confused Mum looked. 'Stop it!' I said. Because I thought this was outrageous. Billie was acting just like Robert's mother. Robert got a Five for Maths at school, a really bad Five. And then he worked and worked at Maths, and tried very hard, and got a perfectly good Four at the end of next term. And when he proudly told his parents about this perfectly good Four, his mother didn't congratulate him, oh no! She gave him a long lecture on how he could easily have got a Three (Satisfactory) or a Two (Good), if he'd worked even harder.

I mean, if someone's trying hard, whether it's a child or a parent, I think you ought to appreciate the fact that they *are* trying, and not go on about the things they still haven't got right!

All things considered, however, it was a really nice week apart from this. If there actually is such a thing as a harmonious family life, then it was a bit of that I felt we had that week.

Saturday, 8th August
Sunday, 9th August

We packed to go away on holiday. We were going to drive round Austria, staying a few nights in various places. Mum took Jasper to buy new swimming trunks, and some flippers, and Dad bought him a beautiful case. Metal outside and lined with velvet, with lots of separate compartments and lockable containers, for his collection of stones.

Jasper was speechless with pleasure. He had a bath on Saturday and on Sunday, to show Dad how pleased he was. And he picked up almost all the used tissues he'd dropped on the floor.

On Sunday evening he asked me why my parents had changed so much. I couldn't very well say, 'It's because they were so shaken up when they heard your unhappy life story,' so I said, 'Oh, it always takes them a bit of time to reveal their true charm!'

'Same here!' said Jasper, grinning.

JASPER'S SECOND THREE WEEKS

Monday, 10th August
Tuesday, 11th August
Wednesday, 12th August
Thursday, 13th August
Friday, 14th August

We spent the first five days of our holiday by the Attersee. The sun shone everyday, but the lake was freezing cold all the same. Jasper didn't mind. He spent hours in the water with his snorkel and flippers. We went sailing too, with a friend of Dad's who has a big sailing boat. Jasper enjoyed sailing. He told us that when he's grown up and his father is dead, and he's inherited his father's money, he's going to buy a sailing boat and live on the water the whole time. And he'll grow a long beard.

All the hotel staff called him Jasper Ketchup, because he wouldn't have anything to eat at meals except three servings of chips and a bottle of ketchup. He didn't even like the hotel fish, though it was very nice. Mum said she thought Jasper must have something wrong with his taste buds. 'The fish he liked best of all,' she said, 'was the fish I burnt under the grill by mistake!' He did have some odd tastes. For instance, he'd put a bag of boiled sweets first into water, and then in the sun on the hot metal of the hotel window sill, until they were a sticky mess. Then he would put this mess in the fridge in the hotel room to solidify. Then, and only then, he ate it with relish. And he liked putting six spoonfuls of apricot jam in his milk at breakfast. And he added sugar to the eighth of a litre of beer Dad let him have at supper. (Mum was not in favour of giving Jasper beer, but Dad said she needn't worry: the filling she makes for her nut strudel at home contains so much rum it must have more alcohol per slice than an eighth of a litre of beer.)

On Thursday we were going to go for a sail, and Jasper was taking his metal case, because Dad's friend was interested in his stones.

I still don't know how what happened next did happen! Billie, Jasper and I were standing in the hotel lobby. Jasper had his metal case at his feet. We were waiting for Mum and Dad to come down from their room. There was a little boy in the lobby too, playing with a rubber ball. The ball came over our way, and Jasper stopped it and was going to throw it back. Then, thinking the little boy couldn't catch it from such a distance, he went a few steps closer to him before throwing it. The little boy caught it. Billie and I said, 'Well caught!' and the little boy threw it back. To me this time. And I threw it back to him. But all this can't have taken more than a minute. When we looked away from the little boy again, the metal case was gone. We searched everywhere. It was no use. Billie kept saying, 'But who'd go stealing stones? I mean, it's crazy!'

Jasper sat down on one of the big leather chairs in the lobby and cried quietly. He cried so much that even his stomach got wet. Then Mum and Dad came down. Mum said it was no use searching. The thief wouldn't have known the case was full of stones, and it was a de luxe case, the sort of thing you might expect to hold, say, expensive photographic equipment. That's the sort of stuff the thief would have been after, Mum said.

Jasper was so miserable that he let Mum stroke his hair, and sobbed in her arms with his face buried in her bosom. There was a great commotion in the hotel, and soon everyone was searching for Ketchup's case. Jasper didn't even notice. 'I wish I was dead!' he kept muttering into Mum's bosom, and Mum stroked his hair and murmured, 'Oh no, my dear, oh no!'

This went on until Dad said firmly (and for this I'm almost ready to forgive him his dreadful English), 'Jasper, my honourword! We drive first off, when all stones are back!' Meaning we wouldn't leave until Jasper had all his stones again. Then Jasper stopped crying, and he blew his nose and wiped his eyes on the sleeve of Mum's dress.

We didn't go sailing that evening after all. Dad, Mum, Billie, Jasper, I, Dad's friend, his wife, her brother and several hotel guests who were perfect strangers except that we'd met them at breakfast, sat in the hotel lounge and composed the following appeal:

S.O.S.!

An aluminium case measuring 60 by 40 by 20cm has disappeared from the lobby of the Schafberg Hotel. Its contents, a collection of stones, are of no value to anyone but the owner, a fourteen-year-old English boy. (But they have great sentimental value for him!)

We appeal for this case, which was probably taken by mistake, to be returned to the Schafberg Hotel as soon as possible. If the person now in possession of the case cannot part with it, would he be kind enough to return the contents in some other container?

Jasper translated this document into English, my father's friend's wife translated it into French, my father's friend's wife's brother translated it into Italian, and the hotel porter translated it into Dutch. In case the thief was a foreigner. Mum typed the appeal out in all these languages on the hotel typewriter, and Dad made piles of copies on the hotel copier.

By now it was quite late, but we set out in four cars. Wherever we went we handed out leaflets. In pubs and hotels and restaurants, in discos, on the street, all round the lake. We stuck leaflets on shop windows and shutters. We even left leaflets on haystacks and farm buildings beyond the lakeside road. If it hadn't all been so sad because Jasper was miserable, it would have been a lot of fun.

We got back to the hotel about midnight, worn out.

'We made, what we could,' Dad told Jasper in English, to comfort him, 'and tomorrow I think what other out!' He meant we'd done what we could and he'd think of something else tomorrow.

But he didn't have to 'think what other out' next day. A chambermaid found the aluminium case outside the hotel door first thing in the morning. There was a little bag hanging from the handle. It contained a note saying, 'Sorry!' and two stones. One was flat and pink, with white markings, and the other was oval, dark grey with a white stripe across it. Jasper was so happy he couldn't speak for ages. And Mum said, 'Well, there are still honest thieves about after all!'

We left the lake, drove to Salzburg and had ice cream at Tomaselli's. Jasper never let go of his case. He even considered tying it to his wrist.

At mid-day we drove on to Innsbruck. It was terribly hot in the car; you could have cooked pancakes on the back shelf.

Jasper asked me if it was far from Innsbruck to Rome.

'About a thousand kilometres,' I said. 'Why?'

Jasper made out he didn't have any special reason to ask.

In Innsbruck we saw the Goldenes Dachl, a gilded roof over a balcony which is a famous landmark, and we ate Tyrolean bacon dumplings. Jasper provided himself with three bags of chips in advance, and he ate the contents of a whole plastic bottle of mustard, because they didn't have any ketchup in the bacon dumpling place. Billie was moaning because she didn't want to stay in Innsbruck. She didn't want to go on to Vorarlberg either. She wanted to go over the Brenner Pass to Bolzano. 'It's prettier there,' she said. But I know Billie. She really wanted to go to Bolzano to look at shoes and dresses. She likes Italian fashions. Mum said she wouldn't mind going to Bolzano either. Probably because of the fashions too.

Dad and I did not want to go over the Brenner Pass. Because we know what *that* means! It means we have to spend hours standing looking at window displays of sweaters and trousers and sandals with Billie and Mum. And waiting inside or outside shops until they've decided what to buy.

So it was two against two, and in our new democratic

mood we decided it all depended on Jasper. Jasper asked if Bolzano was closer to Rome than the Tyrol and Vorarlberg.

When we said yes, he said he'd like to go to Bolzano too.

Sunday, 16th August

We looked at window displays in Bolzano. All day. Nothing but shoes and trousers and skirts and sweaters. Enough to make you feel quite dizzy, and more footsore than if you'd been climbing the Matterhorn. (I'd been dead tired in the morning to start with, because not having booked in advance we could only get one double room and one with three beds in it, so Billie and I shared a room with Jasper. His snoring really is fearsome. I've never heard anything like it! He didn't just snore, either, he whined and muttered and grunted as well. Sometimes he almost sounded as if he were crying.)

Monday, 17th August

Billie and Mum went shopping. I don't know exactly what they bought; all I can say is they bought four carrier bags full of it. I know that, because Mum kept counting the bags wherever we stopped for an ice or a coffee or something, to make sure she hadn't left one anywhere.

In the evening Dad, Jasper and I went for a walk on our own. Billie and Mum stayed in the hotel trying on shoes and dresses and swapping with each other. Saying, 'Billie, I don't think this pink one's right for me—would you like it?' Or, 'Mum, I think the yellow sandals do fit a little better now!' (Luckily they take the same size in shoes and clothes!)

Billie and Mum were bosom friends all day. You'd never have believed, watching them busy buying clothes, that they often don't get on together. Mum was being sisterly to Billie—I mean, like the sort of mother who says, 'Oh, my daughter and I are just like sisters!' But if they were being sisters in Bolzano, they were rather dotty sisters, and they were cross with Dad and me for not buying any clothes ourselves. 'It makes us two look like the big spenders while you're the thrifty ones!' Mum complained. It didn't just *look* like that, it *was* like that! And Dad said a few words, in passing, about our holiday budget not being inexhaustible.

Tuesday, 18th August

A night of snoring, and in the morning Mum and Billie suddenly said they wanted to drive on south.

'As far as Florence anyway, darling Dad!' Billie begged. 'Our Art teacher says everyone ought to see the art treasures of Florence.'

(Ha, ha, ha! Art treasures! Armani trench coats, more like! I'll bet my bottom dollar on that!)

When a teacher recommends you to do something—as with that business about the Oxford college—Mum always thinks you should take notice. And she likes Armani trench coats too.

But Dad and I didn't want to go south, because of our skin. That's why we never go to the sea on holiday. We get itching red spots all over in the heat and bright light of the Mediterranean sunshine.

Mum and Billie dismissed our itching spots by pointing out that the weather forecast was bad. After tomorrow, they told us, it would be neither sunny, bright nor hot in Florence.

You could see their saucer eyes shining greedily at the thought of Armani and Fiorucci and Laura Spagnoli window displays.

So it was put to Jasper to decide again, and yet again he asked if Florence was closer to Rome than Bolzano. On receiving a truthful answer, he said he'd like to go to Florence. By now Dad and I were much occupied with the question of why Jasper wanted to get as close to Rome as possible.

Dad pointed out that we'd have to cut our holiday shorter than planned, for financial reasons, and then we drove on to Florence.

Wednesday, 19th August

Florence was very brown. All shades of brown, and this is supposed to be very beautiful. There was no sign of rain at all. Dad and I sat under sun awnings in front of restaurants, scratching our spots. (I mean, we each scratched our own spots.) Jasper stayed with us, because he wasn't interested in trench coats either. Also he was terribly confused, because he kept hearing the authentic sound of his native language on every corner and at every café table. He said you never noticed there were so many English people around at home in London.

Dad was jittery. Partly because of his itching spots, but even more so because Billie and Mum had taken the cheque card with them. We didn't have much cash left, because of the shopping they'd done in Bolzano. When you go shopping with cash, Dad explained, you soon notice your purse getting empty and then you stop spending. But if you only have to show a cheque card and sign something, he said, you're inclined to spend beyond your means.

Today, however, Dad's fears were unfounded. Mum and Billie had worn the shoes they'd bought in Bolzano to go shopping, and by mid-day they were lying on their hotel beds groaning, with blisters on their toes and heels. And they had to be driven in the car when we went out for supper. Dad didn't get back to our restaurant until we'd reached the ice cream stage, because it took him so long to find a parking place, so we all had two more small ices, because we didn't want to watch Dad eating and have nothing to eat ourselves.

Once more, Jasper asked how far we were from Rome now. Dad thought it would be four or five hours' drive.

'Only four hours?' asked Jasper, squinting in a yearning sort of way.

'Do you want to go to Rome, Jasper?' asked Mum, and Dad choked on his spaghetti in horror.

Jasper nodded. He hesitated for a moment, and then he took a folded piece of paper out of his jeans pocket. He unfolded it and handed it to Mum. It was a letter, but not a recent one. Jasper must have brought it to Vienna with him, because he hadn't had any letters at all since he came to stay with us. The letter was dirty and greasy, in fact it looked like a well-worn antique, but the date in the right-hand corner told us it had been written on 5th July.

It was a letter to Jasper from Mary. The letter said Mary was well and so was her husband, and they'd moved into a little house a few weeks ago, and Mary was working hard in the garden. And she hoped Jasper was well and not doing 'anything else silly'. And right at the end of the letter it said that Mary and her husband were flying to Rome for a holiday in August. 'We'll be staying near the Trevi Fountain,' said the letter. 'I'll throw a coin in the fountain for you every day, and then all your wishes will come true!'

We read this letter. We didn't know what to say. You see, Jasper had never told us about Mary, so we weren't really supposed to know who she was. From the letter, you might have thought Mary was an aunt of Jasper's, or a grown-up cousin.

So Mum asked, 'Who's Mary?' pretending not to know.

'My mother,' said Jasper. He was positively scowling at us as he said this. It was a long time since he'd looked like that.

'Then who is Mrs Pearson?' asked Dad cautiously, like a lion-tamer in the lions' cage.

Jasper shrugged his shoulders. 'Well,' he said, 'she had me when I was a baby, but I don't love her and she doesn't love me. She only loves Tom!'

We all nodded, as if these were the most natural remarks in the world.

'Well?' asked my mother, looking at my father.

'All right,' muttered my father. 'I've already got a rash anyway, and it can't get any worse in Rome! But it's no good just going off into the blue!' He said he didn't think 'near the Trevi Fountain' was very definite, as a place to go, and 'August' was a pretty vague sort of date.

We took a taxi back to our hotel, because Dad felt it

would be too much trouble to get the parked car. He said it would take him half an hour to walk to it, and he was bound to lose his way if he drove back to the restaurant. We could have walked to the hotel, which wasn't far, but Mum refused to go barefoot. 'It would look so bad!' she said indignantly. 'I'm not a little girl any more!' (With six big blisters on her feet, you see, she couldn't be expected to walk back wearing her shoes.)

Back at the hotel, Dad got into conversation with the night porter. They looked up all the better-class hotels in Rome which could be described as 'near the Trevi Fountain' in a big book. (They only looked up the better ones because Mum and the night porter agreed that Americans would never stay in anything less than a three-star hotel.)

Then the night porter rang up all the night porters in the hotels near the Trevi Fountain. This took quite a while, because apparently Italian telephone lines are never very good. Sometimes the night porter had to dial a dozen times before he got through to the porter at the other end, to ask if by any chance Mr and Mrs Max Goldener were staying at that hotel. While this boring and tedious phoning went on, Jasper stood by the hotel reception desk biting his nails, all of them.

I was waiting in the hotel bar with Billie and Mum, drinking tonic water, and Mum was frowning, worrying because she wasn't sure if you ought to go meddling in other people's lives like this. And she wasn't sure we'd be able to track down Mr and Mrs Max Goldener either. 'What exactly does "near the Trevi Fountain" mean?' she said. 'After all, last year we booked into that place that said it was beside the lake, and it took us hours to walk down to the water!'

However, the night porter was successful. After only an hour, he got a night porter on the other end of the line who did have Mr and Mrs Max Goldener staying at his hotel, but they were out at the moment. Dad gave the porter in Rome a message for Mary Goldener, to say we were in Florence with Jasper, who would like to see her, and would it be all right if we came on to Rome? He added our name, and the hotel telephone number. The night porter in Rome promised to write all this down and leave a note with the Goldeners' room key in their pigeon hole.

It was tough going, surviving that night with Jasper. The three of us were sharing a room again. Jasper didn't snore this time, because he didn't go to sleep. He talked instead. He talked more than he'd talked in all the time he'd been with us. He told us how beautiful Mary was, and how nice, and good, and altogether marvellous. He probably wouldn't have to go back to England at all now, he said. First he'd go back to Vienna with us, and then he'd be flying to America with Mary when she'd finished her European holiday. Because he was over fourteen now, and you can say which parent you want to live with once you're over fourteen.

'But she isn't your parent,' I said.

'Yes, she is!' And Jasper stuck to his guns on this point. He said Mrs Pearson had given him to Mary, and when you've given a present you can't take it back. 'She didn't visit me or write to me or anything when I was living with Mary,' said Jasper. 'That's not how a mother acts, is it?'

'But the law—' I said.

Jasper told me he didn't mind a bit about the law. I gave up! I was too tired to argue, and I went to sleep. I woke up once or twice and heard Jasper talking. I didn't know if Billie was still listening or if she'd gone to sleep too. Anyway, whenever I woke up I grunted out loud, so it would sound as if I were still listening with interest. Because it must be awful talking to nobody, just the dark. Billie told me later she'd done the same, but whenever she woke up she took Jasper's hand and squeezed it hard, to show she was paying attention. I couldn't have done that because of the way we were sleeping. I could only have squeezed his toes, because I was on the sofa at the end of the big bed.

Thursday, 20th August

I'll describe this day as briefly as possible, because I still have unpleasant memories of it and I don't like thinking about them.

I woke up when Mum came into our room. She sat down on Jasper's side of the big bed. Jasper sat up with a start and asked if Mary had rung back yet. Mum nodded. Jasper was about to jump out of bed, probably to get dressed so we could set off for Rome directly. Mum held him back. She said, very slowly and very calmly, in German, 'Mary doesn't want us to come.'

Jasper stared at Mum. Mum repeated it in English. Jasper just went on staring. He sat there in bed, perfectly rigid. 'She doesn't think it would be a good idea,' Mum went on. 'She says there's no point in it and it would serve no useful purpose. She says it would be better if you didn't see her again.'

Jasper shook his head. 'You're lying,' he told Mum. 'It isn't true!'

Mum tried to take Jasper in her arms to comfort him, the way she did over his stolen case of stones, but Jasper wouldn't let her. He just went on sitting there, rigid. 'Why?' he asked. 'Why?' he repeated, when Mum didn't answer. She simply looked helpless.

'Tell me!' he suddenly shouted, so loud it made Mum jump.

'Yes, why doesn't she want to see him?' asked Billie. 'I mean, it's stupid! I thought she liked him!'

'Of course she likes him,' said Mum. 'But she says she can't change the way life is, and Jasper is big now, almost grown up, and he must make the best of it. She said if they met now it would only re-open old wounds.'

'You didn't understand,' said Jasper. 'You don't know English all that well! She didn't mean that!'

'Yes, she did,' said Mum. 'I did understand, and Mr Goldener speaks very good German. I spoke to him too. In a few years' time, Mary said, when you're quite grown up, you and she can meet again.'

Jasper still wouldn't believe Mum, so she picked up the phone standing on the bedside table and dialled 8, which put her through to the porter. When he answered, she asked to be connected with the hotel in Rome. And while she was waiting for the call to come through, she told Jasper, 'Mary didn't really want you to, but I think you'd better speak to her yourself.'

Jasper nodded. He put four fingers of his right hand into his mouth and bit the nails. Then Mum seemed to have the porter in Rome on the line, because she was asking to speak to Mrs Mary Goldener. Jasper took his hand out of his mouth and reached for the receiver. Mum handed it over. Jasper held it in silence for a couple of seconds, and then he shouted, 'Mary! Mary!' Then he was quiet again, because Mary was speaking. We could hear her voice, very faintly. A high, chattering voice. I hadn't imagined Mary's voice anything like that.

Mum stood up and signed to us to be tactful and leave the room. We got out of bed and left, with Mum. As we were still in our pyjamas we went straight into Mum and Dad's room next door. Dad was still in bed. He was all worked up, and said Mary was a bitch. 'What harm would it do for him to see her again?' he asked. 'Ridiculous, that's what I call it!'

When I told him that Jasper had been expecting to go to America with Mary, Dad calmed down a bit. And Mum said we didn't know Jasper well enough to be able to say what was best for him. Dad said there *wasn't* any best for Jasper, not the way things were, and the most anyone could do was give him a few little treats. That's what seeing Mary would have been, a little treat.

Just as Mum was saying Jasper must have finished his telephone conversation by now, and we'd better go and see he was all right, the most awful noise came from our room, on the other side of the bedroom wall. Someone was bellowing like a wild bull. As there was no one but Jasper in the room next door, Jasper must be the wild bull. We could hear other loud sounds too. Crashing and banging and thumping.

We hurried into the next room. Dad came too, in his pyjamas. When we flung the door open we saw Jasper sitting on the floor bellowing. The noise was deafening! His open case of stones stood on the floor beside him, and he was throwing the stones. Throwing them everywhere. He must have been throwing other things too. For instance, my jeans were hanging from the ceiling light, and Billie's shoulder-bag was dangling upside down from the open wardrobe door, all its contents scattered over the room. One of Jasper's stones had cracked the mirror on the wardrobe door. Mum ran towards Jasper, and a stone caught her on the shin. She took the case away from him. Deprived of ammunition, Jasper drummed his feet on the floor and went on bellowing. By now there a bewildered chambermaid standing staring in the doorway. And a waiter in a black jacket tapping his forehead. And two hotel guests watching, fascinated. Dad grabbed hold of Jasper and said, in English, 'Jasper, shut up!' Then he said it again in German. Mum rubbed her leg and said, 'Billie, maybe you can calm him down. He's more likely to listen to you!'

Dad carried the struggling, bellowing, kicking Jasper to the big bed, put him on it and held him down. Hesitantly, Billie approached the bed. She bent down to Jasper, about to say something to him, quietly, but Jasper had just wriggled one arm free of Dad's grasp, and he hit out. He hit Billie in the face; not on purpose, though. She didn't bat an eyelash. 'Let go of him,' she told Dad. Mum shut the door of the room, to keep the interested spectators out, and Dad let go of Jasper. Jasper hit out a couple more times, punching the air, then he turned over on his stomach and buried his head in the pillow. Billie lay down beside him and stroked him, very, very gently. She told the rest of us to go out of the room, and said she'd be all right with Jasper on her own.

We went. There was no one left in the corridor outside but the chambermaid.

A little later, we went down to the hotel office in the

lift, for Dad to report the cracked mirror. In the lift, Mum said he'd better ask for our bill too. She didn't want to stay there a moment longer. Everyone in the place would have heard the bellowing, she said. It was all very embarrassing, and she didn't want people staring at her.

Dad paid the hotel bill, and he paid for the mirror, and there was an enormous telephone bill too. He paid by cheque. The mirror was very expensive. Dad doubted that an ordinary mirror could possibly cost so much, but either he didn't want to argue or he didn't dare.

We drove out of Florence about mid-day. Jasper was sitting in the back of the car, between Billie and me. He didn't say a word. He hadn't said a word since his frenzied rage died down. But at least he was reacting to direct orders, like, 'Get dressed now, we're leaving!' and 'Get into the car!' and 'Get out now, please, we're stopping for coffee!'

He wasn't even bothered about his collection of stones. Billie had picked up all the stones he'd thrown around the room and put them back in the case. She carried the case to the car, and Dad was going to put it on Jasper's lap, because he always travelled with his new case on his lap, but he shook his head. So Dad put it in the boot.

We reached Bolzano that evening. Jasper still hadn't said a word. He hadn't eaten anything when we stopped for coffee, and just drank mineral water. Dad planned to spend the night in Bolzano. We tried five hotels, but none of them had two rooms free. Then Mum said she'd had enough of this holiday anyway, and she'd like to go straight home. She asked if we could stand the journey, or would we be worn out by the time we reached Vienna? I said I could stand it, and so did Billie. Jasper didn't react at all.

Mum got behind the wheel, while Dad tried to get some sleep in the passenger seat beside her. Mum shot off towards Vienna, fast. I think she was easily exceeding the speed limit, something she never usually does. She's usually a very careful driver. But luckily there was hardly any traffic on the motorway, anyway, because it was so late.

Somewhere near Innsbruck Jasper's head dropped on Billie's shoulder. Jasper was asleep. And snoring. I'd have liked to go to sleep too, but I couldn't, because Jasper's snores were too loud. So was the car. Our car can go quite fast, but it's noisy when it does. Then, at Salzburg, Jasper's head dropped to Billie's lap, and his snoring was not quite so loud, because he was snoring into her stomach and that muffled the sound. I went to sleep as well. I didn't wake up until we stopped outside our building in Vienna. I was very stiff, and Billie was even stiffer. She said both her legs had gone to sleep under Jasper's weight. Mum said she was so tired she could stay right there and sleep in the car. However, Dad was bright and breezy.

'Slept like a baby,' he explained, stretching.

The sky was getting light in the east as we got out of the car. 'We can take the luggage up later,' said Mum. 'Let's get some sleep first!'

We climbed the spiral staircase, unlocked the double-locked front door, nodded wearily to each other and went to bed. Dad, being so bright and breezy, saw to Jasper: helped him undress, covered him up and pulled down the blinds in his room, so that the sunlight which would soon come streaming in wouldn't wake him.

Billie and I slept till the afternoon. I think it was the smell of coffee coming from the kitchen that woke us. We went into the kitchen. Mum and Dad were sitting there having coffee, and there was some left for us. Mum told us to keep quiet because Jasper was still asleep, and she thought the longer he could sleep the better. And Dad said all we could do now was be nice to Jasper. 'But nice in an ordinary sort of way,' he said. 'Don't overdo it. That would be no use—he'd feel silly.'

Billie and I waited two hours to be nice to Jasper in an ordinary sort of way. I don't mean to say I get premonitions, but I swear that all that time I was feeling something was wrong. I was bothered—something, somewhere, was not quite right. And suddenly, out of the blue, I realized what it was. Jasper wasn't snoring! Jasper asleep but not snoring was plain impossible! I went to his room and opened the door. The place was empty. No Jasper! Several pieces of paper covered with writing were lying on the blue table. They were a farewell letter. It was a mixture of English and German sentences cobbled together, and some of it was so badly written you couldn't make it out at all, especially as he'd been using very thin paper and writing on both sides. The letters from the back of the page showed through to the front and made it even harder to read.

However, one thing was quite clear: Jasper didn't think Mary liked him any more. He thought the reasons she'd given over the phone for not seeing him were stupid and ridiculous. And he thought that now *we* wouldn't like him any more either, because of the way he'd behaved. He wrote that he didn't think anyone would ever like him any more, anyway. He was leaving his collection of stones to Billie, and I could have his clothes. He said he was going away now, to the station. He thought he could find the way all right, and once there he'd change his English money for Austrian money, buy a train ticket, and catch a fast express train. If you jump out of a fast express, he wrote, you're sure to die quite quickly. He hadn't got any poison, and that wasn't a very reliable way to kill yourself either, and if he jumped into the water he'd be sure to swim to the bank. He couldn't imagine a really good swimmer like himself managing to drown. Finally he wrote that he liked us all, and he loved Billie.

Mum and Dad were shaking all over when they'd read this farewell letter. And Dad swore at himself, because apparently, when the rest of us were still asleep and he was sitting in the living room reading the paper, he'd heard a door bang. But he'd thought it must be his imagination. 'I'm a fool!' said Dad. 'I'm an idiot! If only I'd gone to look!'

Mum got dressed and told Dad there was no point in blaming himself now. 'You two get dressed at once,' she told me and Billie. She gave Dad the car keys. 'You drive to the South Station with Ewald,' she said, 'and I'll call a taxi and go to the West Station with Billie.'

Mum rang the radio taxi place, which is very busy on a Friday afternoon. It seemed like ages before at last she said, 'The taxi will be here in a few minutes.'

I was about to leave with Dad when Mum said, 'No, wait! This is no good! Someone has to stay here to answer the phone and keep us all in touch!'

'Who?' asked Billie. I volunteered.

Mum, Dad and Billie hurried out of the apartment, but Mum came straight back, panting. She'd forgotten her purse. 'Don't worry, Ewald,' she told me before she left again. 'We'll soon find him—I'm sure we will!'

I sat down on the stool by the telephone and tried to read the newspaper, but it was no good. I was reading the words and not taking any of them in. Our only hope, I kept thinking, is that Jasper can't find his way to the station. Because if he does get there, I thought, it'll be too late. There are express trains leaving quite often, so he wouldn't have to wait long.

Half an hour later Dad rang. He said Jasper wasn't at the South Station, but he'd told the police, and they were looking out for him. He might be wandering round the city. 'And there's one other likely possibility,' said Dad. A very fast train had left quarter of an hour before, a train with a radio telephone link to it, and they'd phoned the guard of this train and told him what was up, so now he was searching the compartments for a boy looking like Jasper. Another fast train had left half an hour ago, and the people on that train would be told when next it stopped at a station, and then they'd look for Jasper too.

Soon after that Mum called. 'Ewald, darling!' she said, and her voice sounded so happy it was like hearing a chime of bells. 'We've found him!' I told Mum what Dad had been doing, and she said she'd tell the police at the West Station at once, so that the emergency could be called off.

An hour later we were all back together again. There was a funny atmosphere about the place. I think we all acted rather oddly. For instance, Mum asked Jasper if he wanted some grilled fish. I mean, fancy asking people who were planning to throw themselves out of express trains if they want any grilled fish! And Dad read out the television programmes from the paper and asked Jasper if there was anything he'd like to watch, suggesting something that sounded like an exciting film. As for me, I was just grinning stupidly at Jasper. Billie was the only one of us with a bit more sense: she didn't do anything in particular. That night, when we were doing our teeth in the bathroom, she told me she hadn't been at all worried about Jasper. 'I was sure he wouldn't jump out of a train,' she said. 'He just wanted to make us notice how bad he was feeling!'

'You can't know that,' I said, spitting out foam.

'Yes, I can,' said Billie. 'He really *didn't* mean to do it. I looked at the timetable. There were at least three fast trains leaving after he reached the station, but he didn't get on any of them. He was waiting. Waiting for us.'

I thought this over later, in bed. Billie may have been right. All the same, he might have got on a train and jumped if Mum hadn't come looking for him. Because it would have been very difficult indeed just to come back and say he'd changed his mind.

Saturday, 22nd August

Mum sent Billie and me to the supermarket and asked us to stay there as long as possible, because she wanted to talk to Jasper. She'd already sent Dad off to Grandmother's to see if she was all right!

'You see,' Mum told Billie, with a trace of bitterness in her voice, 'I *can* love someone who doesn't behave well! I want to tell Jasper that. I do like him, you know, even

110

though he breaks mirrors and has temper tantrums and acts the way he does! You couldn't feel as sorry for him as I do just because of feeling sorry for him!'

Billie didn't answer. She got the big shopping basket, and was on her way out of the apartment. Mum called after her, 'And I *would* love you, too, even if you smoked hash and stole, and got bad marks at school!'

'Big deal!' said Billie, tartly. But I don't think Mum heard, because we were at the front door by then.

We went shopping, and then we had an ice and discussed the treacherous nature of Life. We discussed Jasper too, and whether Mum had changed this summer. Then, when we saw the two packets of butter in our carrier bags had gone all soft, we went home in case the milk turned sour too.

We found Jasper in the kitchen with Mum. He was eating the frozen fish he'd turned down yesterday. He didn't look too unhappy.

Then we watched television from early in the afternoon until just after midnight. This is very rare in our family. It must have been because we were all so shaken and mentally exhausted.

Sunday, 23rd August

This was a peaceful day. Jasper lay in bed, and Mum brought him mountains of chips, which he ate there. He read that book, *Finnegan's Wake*. I bore Jasper no grudge, none at all, but I did feel slightly aggrieved about Mum. She'd never treat *me* like that, except if I was ill. And when I'm ill she brings me camomile tea, not chips!

But when I said so, she told me Jasper *was* ill, only in

111

his mind, and camomile tea is no use to the mind.

Monday, 24th August

Mrs Pearson rang up in the morning. Mum answered the phone, and then handed Dad the receiver. 'I don't want to talk to that woman!' she told me, quietly.

In his own inimitable brand of English, Dad assured Mrs Pearson that Jasper was 'happy and well up, a good child and high intelligent darling'. Jasper followed this conversation appreciatively, grinning. When he had put the receiver down, Dad whispered to Mum, 'The silly bitch could hardly take it in!' Mum whispered back that he shouldn't call Mrs Pearson names, because you can't tell why people are the way they are. 'That's the mistake we made with Jasper,' she whispered.

Nothing much else happened that day. Except that when I was in Jasper's room, I saw a list lying on the blue table. A list of numbers in red, some of them crossed out:
    ~~22~~ ~~23~~ ~~24~~ 25 26 27 28
And then, in black: 29.

At first I didn't know what the numbers meant. Then I realized that 29th August was the day Jasper went home.

Tuesday, 25th August

I asked Mum if we couldn't keep Jasper with us for good. She shook her head. 'If they wouldn't even let that Mary have him,' she said, 'they certainly won't hand him over to us!'

'But they don't like him,' I said.

'That's what Jasper says,' said my mother, 'but you can

bet Mrs Pearson sees things differently. I'm sure she does love him really, in her own way. Look at us—Billie says I don't love you two in the right way!'

I told Mum not to worry about what Billie said. 'She doesn't mean it like that,' I told her.

Mum sighed. 'And then,' she said, 'there's something else.' She hesitated. 'Another problem, I mean. To do with Jasper. He—' She paused. 'He—' She stopped.

'What about him?' I said.

We were sitting in the kitchen peeling large potatoes for chips as we talked. While Mum was hesitating, and then stopping, Billie came into the kitchen too.

'What's all this about, then?' she asked.

Mum turned the potato she had been peeling round in her hand, examining it as if she had never set eyes on a potato before. Then she looked up and said to Billie, 'He loves you, Billie!'

'Of course!' said Billie, not without pride.

'Not *of course*,' said Mum. 'He wants to be engaged to you.'

'Oh, good heavens!' muttered Billie, and she collapsed on top of the rubbish bucket. She sat there as if it were a very large chamber pot. I'd never seen my sister at such a loss before.

'That was another reason why he didn't want to live any longer,' said Mum. 'He thinks you won't want to get engaged to him.'

'But he's just a child!' said Billie.

'He's only a year younger than you,' said Mum.

'What on earth are we going to do?' said Billie.

'I don't know,' said Mum. 'However, he asked me to ask you if you'd get engaged to him, and now I have.'

113

Billie sprang off the rubbish bucket. 'Didn't you tell him he's too young for me, and anyway—'

'No,' said Mum. 'It was a great mark of confidence from him to tell me what he did. What's more, I'm glad he's still alive!'

'But where in the world did he get an idea like that?' cried Billie, and Mum put a finger to her lips, pointing to Jasper's room. Then she said, 'Well, why shouldn't he get the idea? If he's to survive, he needs someone to love and who loves him back. Now he's lost Mary he's picked on you. Well, obviously he wasn't going to pick me or Ewald for the part!'

I took a deep breath. 'You'd better get engaged to him, then,' I told Billie.

Billie stared at me in horror.

'He's flying home on Saturday,' I said. 'Surely you can stand being engaged for four days!'

Billie shook her head and said that for one thing she was never going to get engaged at all, and for another, if she ever did get engaged it would be to a man, not a child, and the man would have to be exactly what she wanted, very tall with black hair, tanned skin and green eyes.

I wasn't listening to any more of this rubbish, so I interrupted Billie. 'Great!' I said. 'Not so long ago you were telling Mum she can only love well-behaved people, but you're even worse! You can only love good-looking people! Otherwise you'd be able to love Jasper too, just because he *is* Jasper and he wants to be loved!'

'He's off his head,' Billie told Mum.

'Jasper really is leaving on Saturday,' said Mum. 'It's not all that far off.'

'You mean *you* think . . . ?' Billie sat down on the

rubbish bucket again. 'I don't know,' said Mum. 'But it wouldn't do anyone any harm. And it might help him. After all, it wouldn't be a real engagement. As you say, he *is* just a child still, and I think he regards it as a kind of insurance to make him feel secure, if you see what I mean.'

'No, I don't,' said Billie.

'He said that then he'd be related to us,' said Mum. She picked up another potato to peel it. 'I expect I'm talking nonsense,' she said quietly.

'It's not nonsense,' I said. 'Mum is right.' I thought I saw how Jasper's slightly dotty brain worked this one out. It was because he wasn't related to Mary that he hadn't been able to stay with her, and now he couldn't see her any more. So he wanted to set up some kind of relationship with us. That was logical enough. Yes, that would be it.

'You want me to go kissing him to help him feel secure?' hissed Billie. 'You want me to go to bed with him, or what?'

'Billie!' Mum was so shocked she almost cut her finger. 'Don't talk like that! I'm sure Jasper doesn't want you to kiss him, and he certainly isn't after anything more! It's nothing to do with the sort of love you're thinking of!'

'But he wants to come here again next summer, so then what?' asked Billie. She sounded a little less fierce.

'A year's a long time,' said Mum. 'A great deal can change in a year. Where someone like Jasper's concerned, one should be thankful for every year he survives unscathed.'

'Stop going on about it,' I told Billie. 'We'll fry a whole laundry basket full of chips, and grill a whole shoal of fish and get them burnt the way Jasper likes, and use the white tablecloth and have a pink rose on each plate, and I'll buy two rings for you to put on each other's little fingers, and there we are! An engagement party!'

'I'll have to think it over,' said Billie.

'Do that,' said Mum. 'And Billie—if you don't want to do it, then don't. Please don't think I expect you to. It's entirely up to you.'

I really couldn't see why the pair of them were making such a fuss about a feast of fish and chips and swapping a couple of rings.

In bed that night, Billie told me she'd made up her mind. 'I'll get engaged to him,' she said. 'But if he comes back next summer and says now he's fifteen he wants to marry me, then you and Mum can just see about getting me out of it! And let me tell you one thing: I don't want anyone else knowing! If you breathe a word about it in school I'll murder you!'

I solemnly swore not to tell a single living soul anything whatever about the engagement.

Wednesday, 26th August

Billie told Mum she didn't mind getting engaged to Jasper. Mum told Dad. Dad told Jasper. I don't know exactly what he said to Jasper, or whether he told him in English or German. (Afterwards, however, Dad said he'd never felt so silly in his life.)

When he'd had the glad news, Jasper turned up for lunch looking perfectly calm and casual, as if nothing special had happened. He ate a little more than usual, if anything.

That afternoon we went out sailing on the Old Danube. But as soon as we were on the water it began to rain, hard. We brought the boat back. And as soon as we were on land again it stopped raining. We went through this three times, and then we'd had enough of it. We handed in the boat and drove to the Prater.

Dad and Jasper had a great time playing the fruit machines. Billie and I didn't feel like it. We waited on a bench outside the amusement arcade. Billie was quite hurt because Jasper was taking hardly any notice of her. She said it was not the way she imagined people acting when they were passionately in love.

Thursday, 27th August

We had the engagement party. The way it turned out, it was as if we were really all getting engaged to each other! We had masses to eat: not just burnt fish and chips, but cakes and tarts and sausages too. And Dad opened a bottle of real champagne, and we all had a glass.

That idiot Jasper had got an engagement mixed up with swearing blood brotherhood. He was going to cut his finger with the knife he wore at his waist and wanted Billie to do the same, and then they'd put their cut fingers together. But when I gave him the two rings—I'd got them with what was left of the money from my report— he was satisfied with that. Then we sang a great many songs. English songs and Viennese songs, songs from operettas, pop songs, nursery rhymes, all mixed up together. Just as we were rehearsing a round the telephone rang, and the lady who lives below us asked if we'd all gone out of our minds or what? It was only then we noticed the time was long past midnight, and we went to bed.

But Billie and I could hear Jasper singing through the wall. He went on singing for quite a long time. Billie giggled and said her fiancé had a fine baritone. Then she stopped giggling and said in a troubled voice that we shouldn't really laugh, because Jasper was an unhappy person, and the whole thing was very sad.

'Well, it won't do him any good for us to be sad too,' I muttered, and I knocked on the wall. I meant my knock to tell Jasper to stop singing, so the lady who lives below us wouldn't ring again, but Jasper misunderstood. He went on singing and knocked back, knocking on the wall in time to his song.

And promptly the telephone did ring. But this time it was the man on the fifth floor. Dad told him we'd been model tenants for almost twenty years, and he thought it was a bit hard if people came down on us like a ton of bricks the one and only time we did make some noise. Then the man on the fifth floor said he was sorry.

All things considered, the engagement party was a very good evening.

Friday, 28th August

Billie and Jasper and I slept for hours. Mum didn't wake us. (She said later she'd really have liked Jasper to sleep away the whole of his last day with us.)

We got up about mid-day, and Jasper sorted out his collection of stones and packed them. Mum had washed all his clothes. She ironed them, and packed them in the bright green case and the travelling bag. It was a tricky job, because since he arrived Jasper had acquired lots of T-shirts, and his flippers, and a good deal of other stuff.

Dad was out fishing all day, with a friend. He said he couldn't bear such a sad atmosphere, and it nearly broke his heart.

Saturday, 29th August

We drove to the airport with Jasper. As usual, we were hopelessly unpunctual the wrong way round. Even the courier going on Jasper's charter flight wasn't there yet. So we went to the airport restaurant, but Jasper didn't want anything to eat or drink. He gave us his four best stones. Mum was so moved that tears came to her eyes. Dad put his stone, a flat blue one, in his wallet, in the little compartment with a press stud. He said that now his wallet would never be empty, and the stone would bring him luck.

Then they called the London flight. My neurotically punctual mother said, 'They'll call it three times. We needn't go yet!' I was so surprised my ears practically fell off. When they called the flight for the third time Dad said, 'I suppose we must go.' And Mum sighed and said, 'Yes, I suppose we must.'

Jasper let me carry his collection of stones. I really appreciated that.

We handed Jasper over to the courier of the group bound for London. Mum blew her nose. Dad was shifting from one foot to the other. Billie was standing close to Jasper holding his hand. Then he had to go to the check-in desk to hand over his luggage. Billie waited in the long queue with him. I couldn't see the two of them

119

very well, because there was such a crowd in the Departures lounge. Then all the children with the London courier made their way to the passport check point. Jasper was somewhere among them.

'And I didn't even shake hands or say goodbye,' I told Mum.

'Nor did I!' she sobbed. 'I didn't know it would happen so fast all of a sudden!'

Billie wormed her way through the crowd and back to us, rubbing one cheek. She said, 'He gave me three kisses. One for each of you. Want me to deliver them?'

But we don't go in for kissing each other much in our family, so we said, no thank you.

On the way home Mum said, 'Oh, what a summer!' It was hard to tell if she meant a good summer or a bad one.

'Well, anyway, Ewald's made a friend,' said Dad.

And Mum sighed and said, 'But I don't think his English accent has improved!'

Billie nudged me and rolled her eyes heavenwards. She's so hard on Mum. Personally, if Mum and Dad stay the way they were this summer, I'll be perfectly happy. I'll even put up with Mum's craze for people getting good marks! I don't find school work all that difficult, anyway.